S

CHESNEY, Marion
Enlightening Delilah

DATE DUE

31594

STOCKTON
Township Public Library
Stockton, IL

Books may be drawn for two weeks and renewed once.

A fine of five cents a library day shall be paid for each
book kept overtime.

Borrower's card must be presented whenever a book is
taken. If card is lost a new one will be given for payment of
25 cents.

Each borrower must pay for damage to books.

KEEP YOUR CARD IN THIS POCKET

DEMCO

Enlightening Delilah

Enlightening Delilah

Marion Chesney

St. Martin's Press / New York

Library of Congress Cataloging-in-Publication Data

Chesney, Marion.
    Enlightening Delilah.
        p.   cm.
    ISBN 0-312-02912-8
    I. Title.
PR6053.H4535E5   1989   823'.914—dc19   89-30157

First Edition
10 9 8 7 6 5 4 3 2 1

Enlightening Delilah

Chapter 1

*There is great happiness in the country, but it
requires a visit to London every year to reassure
yourself of this truth.*

Sydney Smith

"GOING UP TO TOWN, m'dear," said Squire Simon Wraxall.

His daughter, Delilah, looked at him, startled. "But you never go to London, Papa. You hate it."

"Pressing business," mumbled the squire, picking up his newspaper and barricading himself behind it.

The couple were seated over breakfast in their comfortable country mansion. Early-autumn sunshine shone through the diamond-shaped panes of the latticed windows and sparkled on the silver on the table. The coffee urn on the sideboard hissed like a cat. A fire crackled in the hearth.

"Is it something to do with that letter from London you have just received?" asked Delilah.

"Eh, what?" said the squire. "Yes, yes. That's it."

"And who was the letter from?"

"Fellow about phosphates. That lower field down by the river is in bad heart."

"Put down that newspaper," commanded his daughter imperiously.

The squire reluctantly lowered the newspaper. He looked shifty. Delilah studied him for some moments, and then said, "I don't mind, you know. Mama has been dead for some time. I suppose it was only to be expected."

"Don't know what you're talking about," said the squire, looking puzzled.

"Do not tease me, Papa. That letter was addressed in a very feminine hand. Moreover, it smelled of scent. If you have a lady in London in whom you are interested, then I quite understand."

"I am not interested in any woman," howled the squire. "Mind your own business, Delilah. That's the trouble with women, always gossiping and poking their noses into things that don't concern them."

"Pooh! I am like a clam compared to you. You are a terrible old gossip. Still, if you wish to keep your guilty secret to yourself, then so be it."

She looked at her father hopefully, but he merely said, "Good," and raised his newspaper again.

A small frown marred the alabaster white of Delilah's brow. She rose and helped herself to another cup of coffee and sat down and began to wonder how she would feel with a stepmother. It took her very little time to decide she would not like it at all.

Despite her startling beauty, Delilah Wraxall was twenty-three and still unwed. It was not through lack of opportunity. She had received many proposals of marriage and had turned them all down. She assumed herself to be content with her life. She ran her father's home efficiently. He was very rich and so she could command the latest fashions from London and every trinket her heart desired.

Her father put down the newspaper and got to his feet. "Better be off," he said.

"Won't you tell me who she is?" asked Delilah.

"Now stop that nonsense," he growled, dropping a kiss on the top of her head. "Only be away a few days." He strode out of the room and Delilah heard him calling for his man, John, to bring down the luggage.

The squire really did not think about women other than his daughter very much. Most women made him feel desperately shy. He had been devoted to his late wife, about whom his only complaint had been that she had insisted on calling their daughter Delilah. With a name like that, the squire often thought, one could only expect trouble. For Delilah Wraxall was a hardened flirt. Even at the great age of twenty-three, she was still stunningly beautiful with a white skin, jet-black hair, and large hazel eyes fringed with silky lashes.

There was a rumbling of wheels as the squire's travelling carriage was brought round to the front of the house. Delilah went out onto the step and watched her father as he gave orders to the coachman.

At the age of fifty, he was still a well-set-up man, six feet in height, and with a rather battered handsome face. His hair was snow-white but so thick and glossy that people often assumed it was a spun-glass wig. His eyes were very blue, wide and childlike.

After he had driven off, Delilah went back indoors to put on a warm cloak. She would go for a walk and try to

3

think what she was going to do should her father bring home a bride.

As his carriage jolted along the road to London, the squire took out that letter and read it again. The Misses Tribble, twin sisters who claimed to be able to bring "difficult girls" out at the Season and to find them husbands, had written to say they would grant him an interview. He had appealed to them in desperation after Delilah had turned down her last beau. It was not natural for such a beautiful girl as Delilah to remain unwed. The squire thought his neighbours blamed *him* for her unmarried state, believing him to be keeping her unmarried so as to have an unpaid housekeeper. He would have been very upset had he known that his neighbours all considered Delilah a terrible flirt, a minx, and pitied him accordingly.

The squire was very much at ease in the country, particularly with his farm labourers and tenant farmers. He was passionately interested in all the latest innovations in agriculture and stock breeding. As Town approached, he began to feel like a country bumpkin. He was frightened of women. The fact that he was about to enter into a business arrangement with two of the creatures made him shudder. He wondered for the hundredth time what these Tribble sisters would be like, and for the hundredth time conjured up a picture of two mondaine, fashionably dressed ladies with hard stares and painted faces who would make him feel like a rustic.

"In the name of a whoreson's bastard, will you come downstairs or not?" yelled Amy Tribble.

4

Her sister, Effy, raised her hands to cover her ears. "Don't swear and rant and shout, Amy," she said weakly. "I do not know why you cannot handle this matter yourself. He is only a country squire. I wrote the letter to tell him to come to London. You can surely do the rest."

"If he were a duke or a lord, you'd be knocking me over in your haste to get downstairs," said Amy. "It's because he's only a squire that you have decided it's not worth your time. We were near starvation not so long ago, and could be again."

The Tribble sisters had indeed been on the verge of ruin before they, with the help of their nabob friend, Mr. Haddon, had thought up a scheme to reform difficult girls and make them marriageable. So far, they had had two successes.

The Tribbles were very different in manner and appearance. Amy was tall and bony and flat-chested with great hands and feet. She moved awkwardly and was forever falling over things. Effy was small and dainty with white hair, a pink-and-white complexion which was nearly all her own, and a neat figure.

They were both rumoured to be in their early fifties. In an age when people did not live very long, Amy and Effy could be expected to be planning their funerals. But both still dreamt of marriage as they had dreamt of marriage down the loveless and spinster years. Behind the wrinkles and the fading eyesight, both had hearts as young as they had been when they were seventeen and trembling on the edge of the ballroom floor.

They had become rivals for the affection of their old friend, Mr. Haddon. He was to call at five in the afternoon, and Amy knew that that was also the reason Effy preferred to stay in her room with her hair in curl papers and cream on her face.

5

"You are no support to me at all," said Amy, striding up and down the room. "You let me do all the work."

"That is not true," said Effy, and she began to cry. Amy should have known after all this time that her sister could cry at will, but for some reason Effy's tears always made Amy feel like a brute.

Amy stopped her pacing and looked at the clock. Nearly one! Squire Wraxall was due to arrive any minute. Amy cast a baffled look at her weeping sister and left the room.

She went down to the drawing-room. A housemaid was just finishing arranging bowls of chrysanthemums. Amy shuddered. Chrysanthemums were a new flower, recently imported for the first time and therefore considered fashionable, but Amy thought they smelled of autumn. Another autumn. Another year nearer the grave.

The clocks were just chiming one o'clock when she heard a tattoo sounding on the street-door knocker. She smoothed down her silk gown and adjusted her turban on her grey-streaked locks.

After a few moments, the butler, Harris, threw open the door. "Mr. Wraxall," he announced.

Amy rose to meet the squire, tripping over a footstool as she walked forward, and regaining her balance by clutching hold of his sleeve. She blushed miserably and apologized and then indicated a chair by the fire. The squire sat down gingerly and Amy sat opposite.

"I thank you for your letter, Mr. Wraxall," said Amy. "I will need to ask you a few questions about your daughter."

Harris came in with the tea-tray. Amy looked at the embarrassed and fidgeting squire and told Harris to take away the tea-things and bring in a decanter of the best port.

"My daughter is a very beautiful girl," began the squire. "But she is not married. She is twenty-three."

"Does she have a good dowry?" asked Amy.

"Yes, very good, Miss Tribble."

"Has she had any offers of marriage?"

"Yes, Miss Tribble. A great many."

"I assume, then," said Amy, "that she turned them all down. Why?"

The squire looked at her miserably. He did not like to discuss his daughter with strangers.

Amy looked at his blue eyes which were like the eyes of a troubled child. "This is so very hard for you, is it not?" she said. "But, you see, I feel awkward myself. I am new to business and there always comes a point when I have to bring up the subject of money, and it makes me feel hot and prickly."

The squire studied her. He did not see Amy as she really was—a thin, gawky woman with a face like a horse; he saw only the concern in her eyes and admired her for her direct manner.

He smiled suddenly and Amy blinked. That smile wiped away the years. She thought that Mr. Wraxall must have been devastatingly handsome as a young man.

"You drink your port," said Amy soothingly, "and I will outline what we do. Now, if the girl does not have the necessary accomplishments—by that I mean water-colouring, dancing, playing the pianoforte and so on—we hire tutors. Dress is no problem. We have a resident dress-maker, Yvette, who can make all the latest fashions. If the girl is too wild and unruly, we discipline her. If she is too shy, we train her in self-confidence. We teach the very necessary arts of flirting and conversation. We supply town bronze. You say your daughter is beautiful. Perhaps her head has been turned by too much attention?"

7

"Not quite," said the squire.

"Have another glass of port and take your time," said Amy.

The room was sunny and warm and scented pleasantly with the peppery smell of chrysanthemums mixed with wood-smoke from the fire. There was a good landscape over the fireplace, a view of woods and trees, very like the squire's beloved countryside. Amy was wearing a gown of some dull stuff, but she had a magnificent Kashmir shawl draped about her shoulders, its scarlets and golds adding a touch of barbaric colour. A backless sofa was the one concession to modernity. The chair in which the squire sat had been made in the reign of George II, when mahogany was still a newly discovered wood. It was very comfortable and big enough for his large frame. The other furniture was a pleasing mixture of styles. Each piece had obviously been put there because it was liked, rather than to follow the fashion of having a whole room done out in one of the latest crazes. The Egyptian mode, for example, often led the squire to think the Egyptians must have had a very uncomfortable time of it.

He could feel the tension going out of his body. There was nothing to be afraid of here. He owed it to Delilah to do the best for her.

"This is difficult," he said, "but I will do my best. Delilah was not always thus. I must tell you plain she has become a flirt. When she was seventeen, she was happy, gentle, and kind. She fell in love with a neighbour of mine, Sir Charles Digby, a baronet. Sir Charles was, is, a trifle too old for her. Or so it seemed then. He was twenty-eight. Delilah was very much in love with him. I was uneasy about it, for Sir Charles was very polished, very elegant, and rather haughty and cold. But I admit it all seemed very suitable. He was rich, handsome, his land bordered mine."

"You say 'was,'" prompted Amy. "Did he die?"

"Worse than that," said the squire. "He went up to London. Delilah told me he would call on his return and ask leave to pay his addresses. He returned—in uniform. It was at the height of another scare about Napoleon invading Britain. He called to see me, but not to ask me if he could marry Delilah, but to say goodbye. I suggested he could serve his country just as well by joining one of the volunteer regiments, a part-time soldier, so to speak, but he said he had already made arrangements for his land to be looked after by a steward. I tried to broach the subject of Delilah, saying I thought there was an understanding there. He was icily surprised. He even went so far as to suggest Delilah had been reading too many romances. So off he went. When I told Delilah, she did not say much, but for weeks she was very silent and sad and I feared she would fall ill. I roused myself to take her to balls and assemblies. We may be in the heart of the countryside, but a great deal of entertaining goes on, particularly at the great houses in winter. She began to flirt, at first a little, then a lot. And so it went on. She gained a reputation, but with her beauty, men kept falling in love with her and putting the rumours about her down to jealousy on the part of less fortunate females. If I could be persuaded that her character had changed so much that she had become hard and unfeeling, I would not mind so much. But I am sure she is not happy. That is why I have decided to put her in your care. I know it is a long time until the next Season, but there is the Little Season almost upon us. Do you think you can do anything with her?"

"Of course," said Amy, who actually felt quite dismayed at the prospect. Delilah Wraxall sounded like a horrible girl. Well, hardly girl. She was a woman of twenty-three.

"Then perhaps we can get down to discussing terms," said the squire.

Amy longed to lower their fees. Their usual price seemed like an awful lot of money to demand from a country squire. But then it took a monstrous amount of money to launch anyone on London society. She went to a little escritoire in the corner and began to write busily. Then she sanded the paper and silently handed it to the squire. He studied the figures and then nodded his head. "That seems fair enough," he said. "I will make arrangements for my bank to transfer the money to yours."

Amy beamed on him, relief making her quite light-headed. "And where are you staying in London, Mr. Wraxall?" she asked.

"Limmer's, madam."

"I believe it is quite a comfortable hotel."

The squire shrugged. "Not exactly, but then I never expect to enjoy anything about London."

"Oh, there are many things to enjoy," said Amy.

"The only things I am ever interested in are so unfashionable, I hardly dare to mention them."

A wild thought that he might mean the brothels of Covent Garden crossed Amy's mind for a moment. "What, for example?" she said.

"I would like to see the wild beasts at Exeter Change."

Amy grinned. "Sir, I shall take you there myself," she said, getting to her feet. Amy knew that Effy would adore this handsome squire and felt that by going out with him she was punishing her sister for not doing her share of work.

The squire looked delighted. "I did not come in my carriage," he said. "How do we get there?"

"In my carriage," said Amy. "I rent, you know."

She rang the bell and told Harris to go and hire a carriage from the livery stables and bring it around right away. Then she began to ask the squire about his estates and soon Mr. Wraxall was busily describing the wonders of a new plough which had just been invented in Aberdeen.

By the time they both stepped into the carriage, they were firm friends.

Effy struggled out of bed and looked down from her bedroom window. The squire, looking very tall and handsome, was helping Amy into an open carriage. It wasn't fair, thought Effy furiously. Amy might have sent up word that the squire was handsome. She tugged up the window and leaned out. "Amy!" she screamed.

The carriage moved off.

"I thought I heard someone shouting," said the squire.

"Probably some street urchin," said Amy maliciously.

Two days after her father had departed for London, Delilah Wraxall decided to go for a walk. The day had turned quite warm. She slipped into a serviceable pair of boots, then put an old shady brimmed straw hat on her head and a shawl about her shoulders. She did not look her usual beautiful and fashionable self, but then, there were no hearts left in the immediate neighbourhood to break.

She wanted to go for a long, brisk walk and sort out in her mind how she could find out what her father was up to. She walked through the fields, climbing over stiles, until she reached a path that ran along beside a river. The river banks were thick with trees, which supplied a welcome shade from the sun. Blackberries gleamed wetly in the tangled undergrowth, and one late rose shone in the gloom under the trees. The air was full of the sound of birdsong and rushing water.

Delilah came to a point in the path where her father's estate ended and that of Sir Charles Digby began. She had never set foot in Sir Charles's estate since the day he had gone off to the wars. But that day, she decided to continue her walk. It was silly not to go on. There was no fear of meeting Sir Charles. The war was over and still there was no news of him. His steward knew Delilah by sight and would certainly not dream of accusing her of trespassing. She walked on.

After she had gone a little way, she realized it had been a mistake. Here it was she had walked with Sir Charles, deeply in love, looking forward to a happy marriage. There was the ruined cottage with the mossy wall in front of it where they used to sit and talk. What had they talked about? Delilah frowned. He had talked at great length about the war and obviously followed every report in the newspapers. She had talked about simple things, the books she had read, the dances she had attended, village gossip, things like that. He had never mentioned marriage. But he had sought her advice in the redecoration of his home, had shown no interest in any other female and had stood up twice with her at each of the local balls. Everyone had assumed they would marry. On the day before he went to London, he had taken her walking along this very path and here, under this spreading oak, he had caught her in his arms and kissed her, and that kiss had sent Delilah's heart spinning. She had trustingly told her father to expect a proposal of marriage from Sir Charles.

He had called on her father on his return from London. Delilah had stayed in her room, waiting and waiting to be summoned. She could hear the rise and fall of voices coming up from below. Then, at last, she heard the front door close and, running to the window, had seen Sir Charles riding off. And that had been the last she had seen of him.

There was a fallen log beside the path and Delilah sat down on it. The pain of that rejection came back to her with all the misery of that original blow. Men, she had decided then, and was still convinced, did not have hearts. She would like to think she had inflicted on some of the monsters a little of the pain she had endured, but she knew that any pain would be fleeting. Only women were tender and bruised easily. Although she loved her father dearly, she did not even notice that her flirtatious behaviour was causing him pain.

She glanced at the watch pinned to her bosom. Quarter to three! She would need to return and change. She had promised to take tea with Mrs. Cavendish. Mrs. Cavendish was a widow who lived on the outskirts of the village. She had very little money, but her afternoon tea parties were popular. Everyone delicately tried to increase her larder by bringing along practical presents like tea and coffee.

Delilah hurried home, her skirts flying. She did not have a lady's maid, contenting herself with calling on one of the housemaids for help if she needed the tapes of her gown tied. She put on a muslin gown of apple green and added a new leghorn trimmed with apple blossom on her head. The wide brim shaded her face from the sun. Long gloves of white kid, flat white kid sandals and a parasol of apple-green silk completed the ensemble. Mrs. Cavendish was one of the few ladies Delilah really liked and so she always dressed in her best when going to visit her. She

13

tucked a packet of the finest tea in her reticule and got the groom to load a basket of apples into the gig.

It was a real Indian summer's day. The summer itself had been quite dreadful, rainy and cold. The leaves were just beginning to turn from green to pale gold and hips and haws shone in the hedgerows like jewels.

Mrs. Cavendish had been widowed for some ten years. Her husband had been a gentleman of private means, but on his death, it was discovered that those means had been largely dissipated in gambling. Mrs. Cavendish had sold the large house in which she had spent most of her married life and had moved into a small cottage. She had only one maid of all work and a man who came round twice a week to do the garden.

She was a pleasant motherly woman shaped like a cottage loaf. She was a very good cook and was able to conjure up amazing little delicacies out of remarkably little.

She came to the door herself to greet Delilah. "Tea . . . and apples!" she cried. "You do spoil me. Come into the parlour, Miss Wraxall. The Bellamy sisters are already here, and Patricia, Lady Framley's daughter, and the Misses Peterson. A full house and full of excitement!"

"What is the excitement?" asked Delilah, stopping outside the cottage door to admire the rambling roses which were still blooming at the entrance.

"Nothing to do with me," said Mrs. Cavendish with a laugh. "Sir Charles Digby is returned, and, my dear, what a fuss. All these young ladies have descended on me in the hope Sir Charles will visit too. As you know, he was always a regular visitor in the past."

She saw a shadow cross Delilah's eyes, but the next minute it had gone and Delilah was saying merrily, "I shall not stay long, so that will leave at least one space in your parlour."

Mrs. Cavendish remembered there had once been rumours that Digby was going to marry Delilah. But nothing had come of it and Delilah certainly did not seem to have even noticed his going off.

The Bellamy sisters, Ellen and Bessie, did not look at all pleased to see Delilah. Nor did the Honourable Patricia Framley or Agnes and Josephine Peterson. All the ladies were in their best gowns. The parlour was very small and stuffy, despite the open window.

"So hot in here, my dears," said Mrs. Cavendish. "Let us all carry our chairs into the garden at the back."

There was a great fuss and bustle as the ladies edged out of the back door, carrying chairs. It was a real cottage garden, a riot of late flowers. Mrs. Cavendish was amused to note that the young ladies, with the exception of Delilah, took up Attitudes. Miss Agnes Peterson was sitting with her hands folded on the back of the chair, gazing sternly into space. Miss Ellen Bellamy was standing with hands outspread gazing rapturously up at an apple tree and the rest were in various Attitudes—Virgin Surprised, Spring Awakening, and Stern Minerva. But it is very hard to hold an Attitude for a gentleman who does not appear. Delilah was getting the best of the delicacies, so the other ladies reluctantly abandoned their various poses and joined in the tea party.

At last, Delilah rose to leave. The other ladies looked relieved. And then Mrs. Cavendish's little maid said squeakily from the door to the garden, "Sir Charles Digby, mum."

Delilah turned around so that her back was to him. That one glimpse of him had been a shock. He was as handsome as she remembered him to be, but much harder. There were new lines in his face and that face was brown from the sun.

Sir Charles Digby was a tall man with a high-nosed face

and the odd combination of very thick fair hair and deep-black eyes set under heavy lids. His figure was hard and athletic, his skin unmarked, and his legs good. The fashion for skin-tight breeches and trousers had made every female, however modest, an expert on the beauty of masculine legs.

"You have been away at the wars so long, Sir Charles," said Mrs. Cavendish, "that I fear I must introduce you to these ladies all over again. Some of them would have been in the schoolroom when you left." She led him around the circle and then said, "Oh, and Miss Wraxall, of course."

Delilah swung around and curtsied low. He remembered Delilah as being pretty in a plump, puppyish way. But this was an enchantress who faced him, an enchantress whose large hazel eyes looked green under the shade of a modish hat. She was slim and pliant and deep-bosomed. He realized he was staring, and bowed.

"It is a pleasure to meet you again, Miss Wraxall," he said.

"If only for a fleeting moment," laughed Delilah. "I really must go, Mrs. Cavendish. I have important things to attend to. Goodbye, Sir Charles. Delightful to see you again. Ladies . . . your servant." She swept another curtsy and walked out, with Mrs. Cavendish bustling behind her, pleading, "Cannot you stay for just a little longer?"

Delilah smiled but refused. She climbed into the gig and unfurled her parasol and told the groom to drive on. "Well, that wasn't too bad," she said.

"Beg pardon, miss?" said the groom.

"Nothing. Nothing at all," said Delilah Wraxall.

Mr. Haddon was not a vain man. It never crossed his mind that either of the Tribble twins viewed him in the light of a prospective husband. But he could not help noticing that Miss Effy was not giving him her usual flattering attention. She kept fidgeting unnecessarily with the tea-things.

The nabob had known Effy and Amy Tribble in the days when both were shy young debutantes and he a young man of good family but of very slender means. He had gone to India and made his fortune. But London had changed during the long years of his absence. Only the Tribble sisters appeared to be the same. He did not see any difference in them. To him, they were still the girls who had once been kind to him and who were kind still.

"And you say Miss Amy has gone off with this squire?" he asked.

"Yes," said Effy irritably. "Amy, I regret to say, is a sad flirt."

Mr. Haddon blinked. He could not imagine the forthright Amy flirting with anyone.

"So silly to be over-familiar with clients," complained Effy. "Familiarity can breed contempt. Look at the clock! Where can they have gone?"

"Perhaps he brought his daughter to London and Miss Amy has gone to talk to her," suggested Mr. Haddon.

"Then she should have done no such thing!" said Effy. "She should have sent for me."

"I am surprised Miss Amy did not summon you to the interview in the first place," said Mr. Haddon.

This was where Effy should have explained that she had told Amy to handle it alone, but she did not. Instead she said, "Oh, that's Amy for you. Secretive to a fault."

"I should have thought a tendency to too much frankness was perhaps more a fault of Miss Amy's."

"You don't know her like I do," said Effy darkly.

"I think I hear her now," said Mr. Haddon. Effy flew to

17

the mirror and patted her white hair and bit her lips to bring a little colour into them.

The door opened and Amy slouched in alone.

Effy pouted in disappointment and went back to her chair. "Where is Mr. Wraxall?" she asked.

"Gone back to his hotel," said Amy, slumping down onto the sofa. "What a time we had!"

"Where did you go?" asked Effy.

"He wanted to see the beasts at Exeter Change."

Effy fanned herself vigorously. "How provincial."

"Amazing how all the things damned as provincial are the mostest fun," said Amy. "I had a famous time. Squire Wraxall is a delightful gentleman."

"You really should have called me down," said Effy sulkily. "It's too bad of you, Amy."

"Saw him from the window, did you?" Amy grinned. "I heard you screaming but thought you deserved to be ignored. You know you left me to interview him on my own because you thought a mere squire beneath you."

"That is not true," said Effy, her eyes filling with tears. "Mr. Haddon! I appeal to you. Would I do such a thing?"

"Now, how can he answer that when he wasn't there to hear you," said Amy reasonably. "Do you want to hear about his daughter or not?"

Effy turned her head away and dabbed at her eyes with a handkerchief.

"Please tell us," said Mr. Haddon. "What is the difficulty with Miss Wraxall?"

"She's a flirt."

"Oh, dear, are you sure?" asked Effy, forgetting to be cross.

"Yes. He says some local worthy called Sir Charles Digby raised her hopes a long time ago and then went off

18

to the wars without saying goodbye. After that she went around breaking hearts like a mad thing."

"She must be told that it is not at all the thing to play fast and loose with gentlemen's affections," said Mr. Haddon.

"Doesn't seem to me that a mere lecture would work," said Amy. "I mean a lot of women would play fast and loose if they thought they were beautiful enough to get away with it."

"Not I," said Effy, tossing her head.

"Of course not," said Amy cheerfully. "You never was beautiful enough, so you never even had a chance to try."

"Liar!" screamed Effy, beside herself with rage.

Distressed and embarrassed, Mr. Haddon got to his feet. Both ladies immediately remembered their manners and begged him to stay.

When everything was calm again, Amy went on. "We'll just need to wait and see how she goes on. She can't be all that bad. The father is delightful."

"When does Miss Wraxall come to us?" asked Effy.

"Next week."

"So soon? I trust the squire is prepared to pay our usual fee."

"All signed and sealed," said Amy. "He's awfully rich, and," she added with a sly look at Effy, "he's a widower."

At this, Mr. Haddon insisted on taking his leave. He was afraid the ladies were about to quarrel again. He felt quite upset and huffy and did not know why.

Chapter 2

*. . . I went to London, there to study its
language and its people. The deuce take the
people and their language too!*

Heinrich Heine

AS THE SQUIRE APPROACHED his home, he was stopped several times on the way by various people and told that Sir Charles Digby had returned. This served to harden his decision. All the way from London, he had been dreading breaking the news to Delilah that he had made arrangements for her to be "schooled." What if she refused to go? He could hardly force her.

Now with Sir Charles back on the scene, it was imperative that Delilah should leave. He was driving through the outskirts of the village when he saw Mrs. Cavendish working in her garden and called to the coachman to stop. He jumped down and walked back.

Mrs. Cavendish pressed him to enter her cottage and take tea. The squire felt, on the one hand, that he should return home as soon as possible and get the nasty business of breaking the news to Delilah over and done with, and, on the other hand, he longed for a sympathetic ear. He had always been shy and awkward in Mrs. Cavendish's company, but somehow, his outing with Miss Amy Tribble had removed some of his fear of women.

He soon found himself in her front parlour, sipping excellent tea and munching feather-light cakes.

"And was your business in London successful?" asked Mrs. Cavendish after she had given him the latest village gossip.

Mr. Wraxall carefully put down his teacup and looked at her with worried eyes. "Very successful, ma'am."

"But something is troubling you? Sir Charles Digby is returned and he came here when your daughter was visiting."

"The deuce!"

"Miss Wraxall did not seem in the slightest affected by his presence," said Mrs. Cavendish. "There was a rumour, you know, that perhaps they might marry. That was a long time ago. Could it be that Miss Wraxall refused his suit? She has refused so many others."

"No, she did not refuse him. He, in a way, refused her," said the squire.

"Oh, dear, dear, dear," said Mrs. Cavendish. "Have some more tea. Very comforting thing, tea."

"Yes, I thank you." The squire hesitated. Mrs. Cavendish's round and rosy face was sympathetic. "The fact is," he blurted out, "that I believe Sir Charles's rejection of Delilah was what first began to turn the girl into a flirt."

Mrs. Cavendish searched her brain for the right thing

to say to encourage him to go on. She sensed his need to unburden himself.

"But you have been to London," she said. "Such a pity you could not take Miss Wraxall there for a little. A change of scene is what she needs. I always feel, you know, that she is too exotic a creature to be confined to our small world."

"That's it!" cried the squire. "You see, *I have* been making arrangements. There are two ladies who specialize in dealing with difficult cases. They introduce young ladies to society, and if there is any fault in their characters which is preventing them from finding a husband, then they set about eradicating that fault."

"These are, I trust, ladies of good ton?"

"I only met the one, a Miss Amy Tribble, an excellent woman with great charm and strength of character. Gad, it was so easy to talk to her. Blessed if I can remember talking so freely to any lady since my poor wife died."

Mrs. Cavendish all at once decided that this Miss Amy Tribble was a scheming hussy. The squire should be encouraged not to see such a creature again. But Mrs. Cavendish's kindness and common sense then came to the fore. Mr. Wraxall was sorely worried about his daughter. Something had to be done.

"And so you have made arrangements for Miss Wraxall to go and stay with them?"

"Yes. And now I have the job of breaking the news to Delilah. She will be furious when she learns I am to send her to strangers, strangers who specialize in refining problem ladies."

"Then do not tell her," said Mrs. Cavendish. "It is not at all necessary. Simply describe these ladies as friends and say they have offered to give Miss Wraxall a little holiday in London."

"That's it!" said the squire, slapping his knee. "I'll go right away. You've taken a load off my mind."

"I hope these ladies will be kind to her," said Mrs. Cavendish.

"I have no doubt of it," said the squire. "Miss Amy is kindness itself. A real Trojan. Bless me, I have worried these years about the need for a sensible lady to befriend Delilah. I wish I had thought of this before."

Mrs. Cavendish reflected on all the times she had worried about Delilah's unmarried state, of all her kindness and friendship to the young woman and felt a little stabbing impulse to kick the squire on his backside as he left the room.

The squire felt quite elated as he drove the last lap home. Amazing creatures, women! So sensible if one got to know them.

Delilah welcomed him warmly. Now life could return to normal.

The squire held back his news until they were having supper. He had already had dinner on the road at the country hour of four o'clock, which suited him better than the terrible London time of seven.

"I have a surprise for you, Delilah," he began.

Delilah surveyed him in sudden dismay. Her father looked happy and excited. Here it comes, she thought. A stepmother.

"I may not have told you about the Misses Tribble," said the squire.

"No, Papa, you never mentioned them. Who are they?"

"They are spinster ladies I knew in my youth. Very kind. Live in London. Large house. Best part of Town. I called to see them. As you know, the Little Season is about to begin and Miss Amy Tribble kindly invited you to go and stay with them. Lots of balls and parties."

"And is it Miss Amy you plan to marry?" asked Delilah.

Her father looked at her in amazement. "Gad! I don't want to get married," he said.

"Why did you never mention these Tribble ladies before?"

"Never thought of it."

"And when did you arrange for me to go?"

"Next week."

"So soon?"

"Why not?" said the squire, beginning to become angry. Surely after all his efforts she was not going to refuse.

Delilah put her chin on her hands. "This will take some thought," she said.

"There is no question of thought," said the squire evenly. "I am ordering you to go."

"And if I refuse?"

The squire thought furiously. Then he said, "If you refuse, I shall arrange a marriage for you."

"With whom?"

"Mr. Peter Massingham."

"Do not talk fustian, Papa. Mr. Massingham is three years younger than I. He is spotty. He has a wet mouth. He laughs like water forcing its way down a leaf-choked drain."

"There's always something up with 'em," howled the squire. "You go to London, miss, and do as you are told. You are not going to shame me by playing fast and loose with everything in breeches."

Delilah stormed out of the room.

Never before had her father spoken to her so harshly. She could feel tears prickling behind her eyes. He was a man like all the rest, selfish and unfeeling.

The next day, Delilah and her father avoided each other. The day was again sunny and warm, but the atmosphere in the house was as charged as if a thunderstorm were approaching.

Delilah went out for a long walk, ending up at Mrs. Cavendish's cottage. That lady was as usual delighted to see her.

"I hear you are going to London," said Mrs. Cavendish. "How very exciting."

Despite her distress, Delilah could not help being amused. "How quickly you get the news," she said.

"Mr. Wraxall told me of your proposed visit on his road home last night. Such a good idea."

"I do not like it," said Delilah. "He ordered me to go. He was very angry. He said I could no longer stay here and play fast and loose with anything in breeches. So vulgar! So hurtful!"

"But so true," said Mrs. Cavendish. "Come, Miss Wraxall, you do have a terrible reputation as a heartbreaker."

"I have never broken anyone's heart," said Delilah scornfully. "If the gentlemen choose to make cakes of themselves over me or anyone else, that is their affair."

"And did you not encourage them to do so?"

Delilah got to her feet. "I did not expect you of all people to turn against me."

"I have not turned against you, Miss Wraxall," said Mrs. Cavendish. "Do try to look at it from your father's point of view."

"Why can't he just leave me alone," cried Delilah. "I am happy here."

"Are you?" asked Mrs. Cavendish. "Are you really happy, Miss Wraxall?"

"I was until everyone started saying nasty things about me," said Delilah.

"You have been a trifle spoilt by great beauty," said Mrs. Cavendish. "Your father's only fault is that he should have checked you before."

"I thought you were my friend!"

"Miss Wraxall, pray listen to reason. What is so very wrong and so very terrible about a trip to London?"

Delilah looked at her mulishly. "I shall not go," she said.

As she walked back home, Delilah's furious pace began to slow. It is mortifying to discover that everyone has been talking about you behind your back and criticizing you. For Delilah rightly judged that if Mrs. Cavendish had been shocked at her behavior, then it stood to reason that the less charitable members of the county must have been damning her behind her back for years. She had never once stopped to think about her own behaviour. She enjoyed going to balls and parties and she enjoyed the power her great beauty gave her. A sudden little bright memory surfaced in her brain. The vicar's daughter, Penelope James, had been shyly interested in young Tom Edmonton, son of one of the more prosperous farmers. Tom had been away at Oxford and had written regularly to Penelope. On the day of his return from the university, he had attended a ball in the nearby market town. There, he had seen Delilah. Delilah had begun to flirt with him. She remembered the flickering candles in the ballroom as she laughed and danced with Tom Edmonton and then there came a memory of Penelope's white and pinched face as she sat with the wallflowers and looked at Tom with her heart in her eyes.

Delilah had quickly turned cold to Tom, but the damage had been done. Tom seemed quite smitten. A year later, Penelope had married someone quite different, a much older man who was solidly wealthy.

Tom had left for London to study law. People shook their heads and said it was a great pity, for the young couple had seemed so ideally suited.

"But it was not my fault!" said Delilah aloud to a cow which stared at her placidly over a hedge. "If he really loved her, then he would never even have noticed me."

As she turned into the short drive that led to her home, she saw a light carriage tethered outside the door.

She did not feel she could bear visitors and so she made her way around the side of the house, ducking her head as she passed the sitting-room so as not to be observed. And then she heard her own name and stopped, crouching down among the bushes under the window.

"And so what are your plans, Sir Charles?" she heard her father asking.

"Oh, to look about, enjoy myself, and then return to my duties on the land. Is Miss Wraxall not at home?"

"No," came the squire's voice. "I believe she is out walking."

"I am sorry to miss her," said Sir Charles. "She has become a very beautiful lady. I am surprised she is still unwed."

"My daughter is very choosy and nice in her tastes," said Mr. Wraxall in a heavy voice. There was a silence and Delilah was about to move on when she heard her father say, "I must ask you again, Sir Charles: Before you went to the wars, was there anything in your manner or behaviour towards my daughter which might have led her to understand your feelings towards her were of a warm nature?"

"No, none," Delilah heard Sir Charles say.

You kissed me! she screamed silently.

"I did, I confess, spend a great deal of time in her

company," Sir Charles went on. "I would be most upset if I thought she had misunderstood my attentions. She was so very young and naïve, you see. I fear at that time I could not bring myself to regard her as anything other than a charming schoolgirl, a sort of little sister. She was, of course, not in the slightest interested in the Peninsular Wars, which at that time occupied my every waking thought. She preferred to prattle on about the gossip of the village, but she would nonetheless listen and I needed to talk aloud. I do have a confession to make. Before I went up to London to enlist, I am ashamed to tell you, sir, that I kissed your daughter; but that was all, I assure you. I knew I was going away for a long time and might not come back. I was not only kissing her, but everything about my home and the innocence of the village. Do you understand?"

"Yes, I believe so," said the squire. "And yet, I would rather you had not. You, sir, know that you should never kiss a gently bred lady if your affections are not seriously engaged."

"Come, Squire," said Sir Charles, "and think back to your own youthful follies."

"Alas, I fell in love with my dear wife and never looked at any other woman. You must see, it looks as if you were playing with her affections. You should have thought of the consequences of your action."

"But it did not mean anything to her, surely?" said Sir Charles.

Do not betray me, Papa, prayed Delilah desperately.

"No, not in the slightest," she heard her father say. "I doubt if Delilah will ever take anyone seriously."

Delilah had heard enough. She moved on and slipped into the house quietly and made her way up to her room.

So that was that.

She realized that she had always nursed a dream that

he had really cared for her, that the reason he had gone off without proposing marriage was because he feared he might be killed. But he had seen her as a callow little girl who could only prattle on about village gossip while he worried about the danger to England from that monster, Napoleon.

Delilah waited until she heard Sir Charles take his leave and then she went downstairs to tell her father she had decided to go to London.

The Tribbles received an express from Mr. Wraxall in which he explained he had told his daughter that they were both old friends of his.

"Not very wise," said Effy, shaking her head. "Miss Wraxall is bound to find out the nature of our work sooner or later."

"I should think he had to tell her that to make her go," pointed out Amy reasonably. "Besides, I feel Mr. Wraxall is an old friend. Such easy and amiable manners! I must go to Yvette. She is waiting to pin me."

Ma'm'selle Yvette was the Tribbles' resident French dressmaker. Amy had discovered her among the impoverished French refugees who lived in Kings Cross. The dressmaker had given up trying to persuade Amy that the current craze for girlish muslins did not suit her and had been pleasantly surprised when Amy, immediately after the squire's visit, had commanded Yvette to make two new gowns "which might please the eye of a country gentleman."

When she had gone, Effy drew forward a sheet of writing paper and began to make notes. They would have to find out the limits of Miss Wraxall's accomplishments in order to learn which tutors were necessary. Miss Wraxall would need to be able to sing and play the pianoforte well enough to charm a roomful of London society. She would need to have a portfolio of water-colours to show visitors. She would need a knowledge of Italian and French. She must know how to dance the waltz and expecially the quadrille.

Mr. Wraxall had said his daughter was very beautiful, but fathers could not be trusted to view their daughters with a clear eye. If the girl were so very beautiful, thought Effy cynically, then she would most certainly have been married by now. No woman was *that* hard to please! Now Amy was going to complicate matters by becoming spoony over this squire. Certainly Mr. Wraxall was very handsome, which was more than could be said for Mr. Haddon, although Mr. Haddon was very well in his way. He had all his own hair and all his own teeth. But although he was very rich, his clothes were very dull and sober and he still wore his pepper-and-salt hair tied at the nape of his neck with a black ribbon. So old-fashioned! Nor would be ever wear trousers, always knee-breeches. He was also very slightly stooped, whereas Mr. Wraxall had broad shoulders and carried himself with an air. Effy pushed the list she had been making aside and began to wonder what she would wear when he came to call.

Mr. Haddon could not remember the Tribble sisters being so excited or busy over the arrival of their two previous charges. They seemed to have no time for him. Amy was practically always absent when he called, being pinned or fitted for something. Usually good-natured and sensible, Mr. Haddon began to entertain some petty feelings towards this country squire who had put the sisters in such a flutter.

He felt unwanted. At last, a day before the squire was due to arrive in Town with his daughter, Mr. Haddon announced he was travelling to Dorset to stay with an old friend. Amy, who was dashing through the drawing-room with her hands full of swatches of silk and muslin, looked at him vaguely and said, "Oh, what a pity. You will not meet my squire when he arrives." And Effy started to criticize Amy for saying "my squire" and did not appear to notice.

Mr. Haddon left, feeling very low.

Sir Charles Digby sat in the library of his pleasant country mansion and wondered what to do next. He had made all the necessary calls on old friends and acquaintances in the neighbourhood. His steward had turned out to be a good choice, for everything was in order. Too much in order. There did not seem much for him to do. After the years of fighting, he hated the novelty of being idle. But he had promised himself a short time of leisure and enjoyment.

He found himself thinking of the Wraxalls' sitting-room and how pleasant it had been. There had been huge vases of country flowers, cleverly arranged, scenting the air. There had been an exquisite piece of sewing discarded on a chair and brightly colored silks spilling out of a work-box. His memory of that room with its bright chintz curtains at the windows and the pretty furniture now made his own surroundings seem very gloomy and masculine. He had never got around to those redecorations he had planned with Delilah. The furniture which had served his father and grandfather now appeared massive and heavy, almost as if it absorbed the light. The curtains were of stiff dull red brocade, the colour of dried blood. There was no carpet on the well-sanded floor. The squire's sitting-room had boasted one of those flowery carpets, very jolly and cheerful.

Sir Charles decided that what his home lacked was a woman, a wife. He would like sons and someone pretty to sit with and talk to in the evenings. How incredibly exotic and beautiful Delilah Wraxall had become! An orchid among the English flowers of Kent. He remembered her as she had been at seventeen, plump and pretty and ingenuous, her eyes as wide and innocent as those of a fawn. He remembered talking to her at length and occasionally becoming irritated when it seemed as if Napoleon and all his threat to England meant so much less to her than a new recipe or the latest fashion from London. She had changed outside, but he was sure her mind had not changed. He dreamt of a woman, not necessarily beautiful, but with a clever mind and a certain something to excite his senses. He had no intention of following the example of most of his peers and looking for love and recreation outside marriage. He would expect the wife of his choice to be equally faithful. He thought again of Delilah. Evidently, she had become a dreadful flirt. Sir Charles despised flirts.

No, there was not even one lady in his immediate neighbourhood with whom he would be happy to settle down. He felt restless. The sunny weather only seemed to make him discontented. He remembered he had promised himself an extended stay in London on his return. There were so many plays and operas to see, so many army friends to look up. His best friend, Lord Andrew Bergrave, had pressed him to come on a visit to his fine town house in Brook Street.

"Don't even trouble to write," Lord Andrew had said. "I shall be in London right up until Christmas."

And there were clever and witty and fascinating

women in London society whose minds were surely of a higher order than those of the little misses of the neighbourhood.

Delilah. How his thoughts kept returning to her. The squire had made him feel uncomfortable. He should never have kissed her. But she had seemed so young and endearing and he had been going away and thinking he might never return.

He decided to start arrangements to go to London that very day. No need to tell anyone other than his steward. If the local worthies knew he was going, then he would have to endure another round of calls.

Beginning to feel more cheerful now that he had come to a decision, he made plans for his journey.

Delilah began to feel a certain pleasurable anticipation as the day of her departure drew near. She had never been to London. Of course, the idea of staying with strangers was a bit lowering. She did wish her father would tell her a little more about these Tribble sisters, but he was infuriatingly vague.

She called again on Mrs. Cavendish to make her good-byes.

"So sensible of you to go," said Mrs. Cavendish comfortably. "Everyone should go to London at least once."

"Have you been?" asked Delilah curiously.

"I made my come-out at the Season," said Mrs. Cavendish. Her eyes suddenly became dreamy. "How wonderful it all was. Oh, the balls and suppers and carriages in the Park. What a fuss and flutter I was in, for my parents were expending a great deal of money, you know, and it was my duty to become engaged before the end of the Season. And I was so very dutiful. I would have settled on anyone at all suitable just to please them. In fact, I nearly accepted the hand of old Lord Lissom, who was quite twenty-five years older than I. He had wooden false teeth, quite off-putting. But one must always do one's duty. And then my late husband arrived on the scene. It was at a Wednesday night at Almack's. How surprised you look! But I was staying with my aunt, who was *very* good ton, and she was a friend of one of the patronesses, so I got my vouchers. John, my husband-to-be, asked me to dance. It was one of those hurly-burly Scotch reels where one does not have much opportunity for dalliance or conversation, but we knew then, from that first moment, that we were in love. I never looked back, never regretted it."

Delilah looked at her wide-eyed, reflecting that the late Mr. Cavendish had hardly been a model husband. He had left his poor wife a mountain of debt and she had had to sell her large and comfortable home and estates and all her jewelry to meet the costs.

Mrs. Cavendish laughed. "You are thinking it was a poor sort of man to leave me in such straits, but we were very happy. You cannot do much about gambling, you know. His grandfather was a gambler. The Fatal Tendency missed a generation and then descended on my poor John. It is of no use telling gentlemen not to gamble, you know. They *will* do it."

"But did he never feel remorseful, ashamed of himself?" asked Delilah.

"Well, I suppose he sometimes did. But hardened gamblers are such charmingly optimistic creatures, you know. They are always quite sure that something will turn up to get them out of the mess. Strangely enough, something usually does, but it only makes them gamble harder than ever."

"Did you never wish you had children?" asked Delilah.

"I do now. But, of course, my John was not only my husband but my child as well. He was all I ever thought about and cared about. I fear you are too nice in your tastes, Miss Wraxall. No man is perfect. You must make allowances."

"Perhaps I do not wish to marry," said Delilah. "I do not see why one should if one does not wish to do so."

"Have you never thought that your father might have married again had he not had the care of you?" asked Mrs. Cavendish.

"I never really thought about it," said Delilah, "until recently, that is. I suppose I *should* think about it. He seems quite taken with this Miss Amy Tribble. I imagine she is very beautiful. No, I did not consider such an eventuality. After all," she said with a light laugh, "there is no one in this village Papa could honestly be interested in."

Mrs. Cavendish was normally a happy and contented woman who had come to terms with the narrowness of a life of genteel poverty. But as she looked at Delilah's laughing and beautiful face, she experienced a strong impulse to slap it, and was immediately shocked at her reaction.

There came a knock at the door. Glad of the diversion, she got quickly to her feet just as her little maid announced Sir Charles Digby.

Delilah rose and curtsied.

"You are come just as I was taking my leave," she said.

As if to give the lie to her remark, the little maid entered again with the tea-tray and placed it on a table.

"But you must stay!" said Mrs. Cavendish.

"Please do," said Sir Charles. "I fear I am driving Miss Wraxall away."

"No, I assure you," said Delilah. "I have much to do."

"Just some tea and then you may go," said Mrs. Cavendish. "I have some blackberry jam to give you for your father. You know how much Mr. Wraxall likes my blackberry jam. Now, Sir Charles! Are you settled in among us again?"

Sir Charles hesitated but decided not to say he was leaving. Had Delilah not been there, he would have told Mrs. Cavendish in confidence. She was one of the few people in the village of whom he was fond.

"I feel quite useless," he said with a laugh. "I came back expecting to find plenty of work to do, but on the contrary everything seems to be running smoothly."

"Mr. Jenkins is a good steward," said Mrs. Cavendish. "Will you be getting rid of him now you are back?"

"That was the idea. But he has settled in so well that I do not wish to dislodge him. How do you fare, Miss Wraxall?"

"Very well, Sir Charles," said Delilah. "I see you survived the wars without a scratch."

"I was very lucky. I fear I lost a great many friends."

"It must seem odd," said Delilah, "to return here with all those memories of death and bloodshed, heat and carnage and find us all quietly going about our tedious affairs as if the very security of England had never been threatened."

He looked at her in surprise. "Yes, that is the case."

"Two years ago, I went shopping on market day in Drufield," said Delilah. "It was bustling and cheerful. There were chapmen selling their wares and children darting in and out of the crowds, and acrobats and strolling players and men selling gingerbread. There was a lame soldier begging for alms, moving like a dark shadow among the crowd. People turned away from him. It was not that they were precisely uncharitable people, but sim-

37

ply that he looked so lame, so bitter, so angry that he was about as welcome as a death's head at the feast. Then he cried out, 'I fought for you. I fought for this. My comrades are over there, dying in that dreadful country while you frolic at your ease.' It was quite shocking, you know, such a cry of frustration and pain."

Sir Charles looked at her. "Did you give him anything?"

"Yes," said Delilah, and fell silent. She had actually given the soldier the contents of her purse and so had returned home without buying anything.

He studied her, marvelling again at her extraordinary beauty.

"It is all very sad," said Mrs. Cavendish. "I was at Lady Framley's the other day, and one of her guests began to talk about the war and was shushed into silence. 'Ladies present,' said Lady Framley severely, as if the poor man had said something indecent. And yet, when the threat of Napoleon was at its very height, how everybody did cheer the redcoats!"

"I am afraid the English have always loathed their soldiers except in times of peril," said Sir Charles. "Do you not see the signs outside the taverns now, 'No Redcoats'?"

"There is no fear that monster will escape from that island he is on?" asked Mrs. Cavendish.

"I hope not. But I believe there is still great support for him in France. One wonders why. The country is in a shocking state and there are many women working in the fields because their men are dead.

"Perhaps we owe Russia as much a debt as we owe the great Duke of Wellington," said Delilah. "If Napoleon had not decided to invade Russia, perhaps his great army would not have been so enfeebled. Now, I must beg you both to excuse me."

Delilah curtsied to Sir Charles and made her way out, followed by Mrs. Cavendish, who was shouting to her maid to fetch a pot of blackberry jam from the pantry.

When Mrs. Cavendish returned, Sir Charles was standing by the window, watching Delilah climbing into her carriage.

"Miss Wraxall has changed," he said. "When I knew her, she had no interest in anything other than feminine trivia."

"She has a good mind," said Mrs. Cavendish.

Sir Charles swung round. "I am come to make my farewells, Mrs. Cavendish. I go to London for a few months."

"We are very sorry to lose you," said Mrs. Cavendish. She wondered whether to tell him that Delilah, too, was going to London, but decided against it. Miss Wraxall and her father had not wanted the news broadcast about: Delilah because, like Sir Charles, she did not want to be subjected to a round of calls and leave-takings; and the squire because he wanted to avoid questions about his supposed friends, the Tribble sisters.

"What takes you there?" asked Mrs. Cavendish.

"I promised myself a round of pleasure on my return," said Sir Charles. "Besides, it is time I found a wife and settled down."

"You do us a disservice," teased Mrs. Cavendish. "Are there no ladies among the local belles good enough for you?"

"I think I would like to try further afield."

"Well," said Mrs. Cavendish slyly, "it could be you might meet one of our local ladies in London and fall in love and find you have wasted your journey."

"I doubt it," he said. "But pray keep this news to yourself. I have no desire to have to go the rounds and sit over endless teacups explaining myself."

"I won't breathe a word," said Mrs. Cavendish. She hesitated and then a desire to satisfy her own curiosity and also to find some way of getting Sir Charles and Delilah together in London made her say, "The squire has formed a friendship—or rather re-formed one—with a certain Miss Amy Tribble. She resides in Holles Street. I know we are very parochial here, but the squire is an old friend and I am anxious he is not going to make the mistake of marrying someone unsuitable. Would it be too much to ask you to call on this Miss Amy Tribble and send me a report?"

"I shall be glad to do such a trifling service for you."

After he had left, Mrs. Cavendish thought about Sir Charles and Miss Wraxall. She felt they were eminently suitable. Both had more than their fair share of good looks, both appeared to hold strong views on various subjects. Both belonged to the village, and Mrs. Cavendish felt that people from the village should stay together and not waste their time bringing in foreign blood—by which she meant unknown people from London. Sir Charles would be understandably annoyed with her to find Delilah in residence with the Tribbles, but then, by the time he called, he might be glad to see a familiar face. He was a gentleman and had promised her a letter describing this Miss Amy Tribble, and no matter how high his irritation might be, Mrs. Cavendish knew he would still send that letter. She rose and bent to collect the tea-things. Having only the one maid meant that you had to do a great deal of things yourself. She caught a glimpse of herself in the mirror as she bent over the table. How fat I am become, she thought in dismay. I must start to go for long walks again and not eat so much. Gentlemen like plump ladies, but not when they are so very fat as I!

40

Delilah and her father set out for London on another beautiful morning. The mist was just rising off the fields so that it was like looking at the landscape through gauze. Red and gold leaves fluttered down on the roof of their carriage as the squire's travelling coach bowled through the country lanes to join the London road.

It was a long, easy, golden day of travel. Delilah had brought a novel to read, but the book lay unheeded on her lap as she looked out with pleasure at the glory of the countryside. They stopped for the night at a posting-house and went to bed, planning to set out as early as possible.

In the morning, the waiter banged at the door of Delilah's room and called, "Seven o'clock."

Delilah struggled awake and drew back the bed-hangings. The room was so cold and dark, she thought the waiter must have made a mistake. It felt like midnight. A little chambermaid scratched at the door and then scurried in and began to make up the fire.

"Very cold, mum," she said over her shoulder. "Frost's something bad."

"Frost?" said Delilah sleepily. "But it was so beautiful yesterday."

"Well, that's the English weather, mum," said the girl, as if instructing a foreigner. "No good will come of all this sunshine so late in the year. That's what my father said. He do say his big toe had been aching something awful and that allus means a change in the weather."

When Delilah and her father climbed back into their carriage, the bleak aspect of the countryside bore witness to the infallibility of the chambermaid's father's big toe. Everything was chilly and white under a lowering sky.

There was not even a breath of wind, and smoke from cottage chimneys rose straight up in long lines to the sky. The starlings piped with that dismal descending note they have on cold mornings and the carriage bumped and swayed over the frozen ruts in the road.

They planned to arrive in London by early afternoon. Delilah had imagined a sunny London, a London of fluttering flags and pretty dresses and open carriages. But as they drove silently through the suburbs, the day became darker and darker.

"Fog's coming down," said the squire. "Look, Delilah. Over there! That's St. Paul's Cathedral."

Delilah looked out of the window. A small red sun shone down on the cupola of St. Paul's. But, as she watched, great wreaths of yellow-greyish fog closed down over the famous cathedral and blotted out the sun. Link-boys darted here and there through the gloom of the street like fireflies. Fog penetrated the carriage. The squire lit the carriage lamps inside the coach and the fog lay in long bands in front of their faces.

Now the streets were full of clamour and noise. Unseen beings called their wares, black shapes of carriages lurched through the fog like ships on a dreadful sea, and the cold became more intense.

"I'll need to get out and walk and lead the horses," said the squire. "Jack-Coachman'll get lost in this."

So Delilah was left alone with her thoughts. She wrapped the bearskin rug more tightly about her knees. Behind her she had left a sunny, happy world. Why had she agreed to come to London? She hated it already. It would have been fun to stay and demonstrate to the haughty Sir Charles how little she cared for him, how little she had ever cared for him.

Now, it was too late. By the time she returned, he

would probably be engaged to someone like Bessie Bellamy. Delilah briefly thought of how Bessie would queen it over everyone else should such a thing happen, and then fell to wondering again about Miss Amy Tribble and whether her father could be thinking of marrying again.

Chapter 3

Of all the torments, all the cares,
With which our lives are cursed;
Of all the plagues a lover bears,
Sure, rivals are the worst!
By partners in each other kind,
Affections easier grow;
In love alone we hate to find
Companions of our woe.

William Walsh

DELILAH WAS LONG TO remember that last stage of the journey to Holles Street. The carriage inched forward through the suffocating gloom. Occasionally the fog would thin slightly to show the blurred yellow light of a shop window with black silhouettes of people standing in front of it.

She began to feel apprehensive. As the squire's daughter, she had been queen of the little community in Kent. Now she was just a provincial being slowly swallowed up into the vast gloom of London.

She began to hope that her father had lost the way. They would put up at some hotel where she could persuade him to take her back home in the morning.

Then, after a longer stop than usual, her father opened the carriage door and said, "We are arrived, Delilah."

She climbed down stiffly. Her father took her arm and led her up the steps of a mansion.

There was a very grand liveried butler holding open the door.

He bowed and said, "The Misses Tribble are awaiting you in the drawing-room. Please follow me."

Harris, the Tribbles' butler, led the way up a curved staircase to a room at the top on the first floor. He threw open the double doors and announced, "Mr. Wraxall and Miss Wraxall."

The squire and Delilah entered. Two ladies rose to meet them. Delilah's eyes flicked over the tall flat figure of Amy and came to rest on Effy. Effy's white hair gleamed like silver. She was wearing a lilac silk gown covered with a gauze scarf of deeper lilac. Her face had a delicate faded prettiness. In her hand she held a painted fan which she raised to her face and batted her eyelashes at the squire over the edge.

"We have not met," said Effy. "I am Miss Effy Tribble. You have, I believe, already met my sister, Miss Amy."

Delilah concealed her surprise. So the other one was Miss Amy. Amy was wearing a scarlet merino gown, beautifully cut. On her head was a scarlet velvet cap trimmed with gold. She had the face of a rather sad, tired horse.

"This is my daughter, Delilah," said the squire. Delilah curtsied. "Come and sit by the fire," said Effy. "You both

46

must be frozen. We were going to offer you champagne before that freezing fog came down, but I think a bowl of punch will be more the thing."

Two footmen came in with a punch-bowl and all the ingredients and placed them on a table. Amy set about making the punch. "Always do it myself," she said with a grin at Delilah. "Servants never make it strong enough."

That grin altered Amy's face. Delilah's heart sank. Miss Amy Tribble had a certain direct charm. But she also looked formidable, the sort of stepmother who would not appreciate having another woman running the household.

"Sit down by me, Mr. Wraxall," cooed Effy, "and tell me all about your journey."

Amy glared at her sister and poured a whole bottle of brandy into the punch-bowl. Amy knew Effy had a weak head for spirits.

The squire was not at ease with Effy. Her flutterings and sly glances made him feel hot and awkward and miserably aware that the linen of his cravat was speckled with soot.

Amy poured glasses of punch and a footman took them round. Delilah nearly choked over hers, it was so strong, but soon the punch began to spread a warm glow throughout her body.

"I hope you plan to spend a few days in Town, Mr. Wraxall," said Amy, sitting down on the other side of him from Effy.

"I plan to leave the day after tomorrow," said the squire.

"Have you ever been to Astley's Amphitheatre?" asked Amy.

"Terrible place," interrupted Effy with a delicate shudder. "I detest circuses. Full of low people."

"I have never been," said the squire, "but I've always

longed to go." He looked apologetically at Effy. "I fear I do not have very sophisticated tastes, as Miss Amy well knows."

"I took the liberty of getting us tickets for tomorrow night," said Amy cheerfully. "That is, if you would care to accompany me, Mr. Wraxall."

The squire's blue eyes lit up. "I should be honoured and delighted to go, Miss Amy."

"Amy!" said Effy sternly. "You are surely not thinking of starting Miss Wraxall's début in London at Astley's!"

"Not I," said Amy. "I only bought two tickets. I have the same unsophisticated tastes as Mr. Wraxall."

Effy drank another glass of punch. "And what am I supposed to do with Miss Wraxall?"

"Begin her education, if you like," said Amy and then coloured as the squire flashed her a warning look.

"What education?" demanded Delilah. "I am long out of the schoolroom."

"But you have not been in London before," said Effy. "You need town bronze."

"We have many notables who attend our local parties and assemblies in the winter," said Delilah. "I know very well how to go on."

"We shall shee," said Effy, and then looked in a surprised way at her glass as if it had slurred rather than herself.

"Sush a pity Mr. Haddon is not here," went on Effy. She turned to Delilah. "My shishter is monshtroushly taken with Mr. Haddon."

"I think you have had too much punch," said Amy crossly. "You're making noises like a crossing sweeper's brush."

"Who is Mr. Haddon?" asked the squire hurriedly.

48

"An old friend of *ours*," said Amy. "Effy hopes to marry him."

"I do not," said Effy. "You are the one who ish always making a cake of yourshelf over him. You—"

"Oh, do shut up, Effy," said Amy. "You're drunk!"

Effy burst into tears while the squire and his daughter exchanged looks of acute embarrassment. Amy rang the bell and a stern-faced maid answered it. "Baxter," said Amy, "Miss Effy is a trifle overcome. Take her to her room."

Baxter looked at the punch-bowl and then went and helped the sobbing Effy to her feet.

There was a long silence after they had left the room. Then Amy said, "You must have supper. Did you dine on the road?"

"We had quite a large dinner at four," said the squire. He felt uncomfortable and wanted to leave, but he could hardly abandon Delilah so quickly. He was regretting his decision to turn her over to the Tribbles.

Amy read that indecision in his face and set herself to please. The Wraxalls were conducted upstairs to wash and change.

The supper was excellent and Amy encouraged the squire to talk. Delilah had never heard her father chatter on so much to any lady. Usually he was silent and let his daughter make most of the conversation.

Delilah had sensed earlier that her father was in two minds about leaving her. But by the end of the supper party, she knew he was once more happy with Miss Amy Tribble.

She felt gauche and ill at ease. In the village, everyone had deferred to her, even Lady Framley and her daughter. But she knew that in Amy's eyes, she was important only because she was the daughter of a handsome widower.

49

Neither Amy nor Effy had remarked on her beauty, and Delilah, who thought she did not care for perpetual compliments on her appearance, now sorely missed the lack of them.

She clung to her father as he stood in the hall, taking his leave.

When he had left, Amy turned Delilah over to Baxter, the lady's maid, who took her up to her room and prepared her for bed. Delilah was not used to the services of a lady's maid, a luxury she could easily have afforded but had not considered important, and found it pleasant to have her hair brushed and a glass of hot milk handed to her, and to have all her fog-soiled clothes taken away to be sponged and pressed.

Delilah awoke next day to the sounds of a furious altercation coming from somewhere belowstairs. Then she heard Amy shout, "A pox on you and your humours, Effy. It is your own fault if you cannot hold your drink!"

What an odd pair, thought Delilah, bewildered. Is this how London society goes on?

A chambermaid came in and drew the curtains back. "Fog's gone, miss," she said. "It's a lovely day." Sunlight streamed into the room.

The chambermaid left after lighting the fire and was shortly followed by Baxter, who began to look through the contents of Delilah's wardrobe. She examined the boning in Delilah's dresses and shook her head. "I'll need to get that Frenchie dressmaker to look at these, miss," said Baxter. "No one wears them like this any more. Unnatural the way they push up the breasts so."

"I had these gowns made for me in London," said Delilah.

"Ah, well, you wouldn't know any better, miss," said Baxter. "Who made these?"

"Mr. Treadwell."

"No one uses Treadwell any more," said Baxter. " 'Cept dowagers, that is. Better to have a woman design things for you anyway. Men are always behind the times."

She selected a gown of blue tabinet and then set about preparing Delilah for the day ahead and arranging her hair in one of the new styles.

When Baxter considered she was ready, Delilah was conducted down to a morning room where Effy was sitting alone, having breakfast.

"How beautiful you look, child!" said Effy. "Pray be seated and tell Harris what you want."

Delilah ordered cold ham, eggs and kidneys, toast and coffee.

"How do you keep your figure?" sighed Effy. "Dry toast is all I allow myself. But then I eat like a bird. I must apologize for my illness last night. I am not strong, you know. Now, if you consider yourself rested, we shall make some calls this afternoon to introduce you to various people."

"Will not my father be calling?" asked Delilah.

"He *did* call, but he has gone out driving with my sister. We shall no doubt see both of them later in the day. Now, let us check your accomplishments. Do you play the pianoforte?"

"Yes, but not very well."

To Delilah's surprise, Effy drew out a small notebook and pencil and wrote "music teacher" in it.

"Italian and French?" asked Effy.

"A very little," said Delilah.

"Dear, dear, dear. Italian and French tutors," said Effy, writing busily. "Needlework?"

"I embroider well."

"That's something, I suppose," said Effy. "Watercolours?"

"I am accounted very good."

"Singing?"

"Fair."

Effy's pencil hovered over the paper of the notebook. "Perhaps not," she murmured. "Unnecessary expense. Dancing?"

"Yes, I dance," said Delilah.

"Waltz?"

"Yes."

"Quadrille?"

"No."

"Dancing master," said Effy, writing it down. "Would you mind walking up and down the room for me, Miss Wraxall?"

Torn between amusement and exasperation, Delilah pushed away her plate, got up and walked slowly up and down.

"Not bad, not bad," said Effy. "But bridle. You must bridle. You tuck your chin in and look down your nose . . . so."

Delilah burst out laughing. "That looks silly."

"There is a great deal in London society which looks silly," said Effy repressively, "but one must strive to please. Harris," she said to the butler, "we shall need a dancing master, music teacher and French and Italian tutors. Deportment can be taught by ourselves."

"It is very kind of you, Miss Effy," said Delilah, "but why are you going to such an effort to school me? I am only here for a short time and then I shall return to the country."

Effy remembered in time that they were supposed to be old friends of the squire. "It is always important to be good ton," she said.

"On whom are we to call?" asked Delilah.

52

"I think we shall call on the Marchioness of Raby. She is very *comme il faut*. You must study her manners and aim to copy them. Harris, bring me the card rack from the drawing-room." She waited until the butler returned and placed a little rack containing a great many gilt-edged invitations and began to look through them.

"Now, here, next week is a ball and quite a grand one, too," said Effy thoughtfully. "Lady Burgoyne. I said we should not attend, but I am sure she will understand if we explain you are newly arrived from the country and we wish to puff you off and plan to come after all. And, let me see, there is a musicale on Wednesday . . . perhaps . . . and a turtle dinner. Yes, we shall go on very well. Harris, send for Ma'm'selle Yvette."

Delilah sat feeling bewildered. Perhaps it was the London fashion to school young guests. The French dressmaker came in and Effy instructed her to look over Delilah's wardrobe and alter anything that needed altering. "In fact," said Effy, "take her with you and pin her."

"May I finish my breakfast first?" asked Delilah.

"Yes, of course, child. But not too much heavy food. You will have spots all over your face in no time at all."

The Marchioness of Raby lived in a pretty town house in Bolton Street. She was small and dumpy with a round head and a very large mouth. She had tried to reduce the size of her mouth by painting a small pair of lips in the centre of her own. This, combined with the amount of white lead she wore on the rest of her face, contrived to give her the appearance of a clown. She welcomed Effy with great enthusiasm and offered Delilah only the curtest of nods and two fingers to shake.

She then drew Effy down beside her on the sofa and

began to chatter, leaving Delilah completely ignored. Then a Mrs. Busby and her married daughter, Mrs. Tomlinson, were announced. Mrs. Busby, like the marchioness and Miss Effy, looked to have reached her half-century, but she was dressed in damped muslin which revealed she was wearing the latest in corsets, called The Divorce, because it was the first piece of corsetry ever invented that separated the breasts, rather than presenting them as one solid front.

Mrs. Tomlinson was heavily pregnant and made no attempt to hide that fact. Delilah saw that these newcomers were about to ignore her as well and was determined to enter the conversation. She smiled at Mrs. Tomlinson and said, "When is your baby expected?"

There was a shocked hush. The marchioness turned red with embarrassment under her paint, and then Effy, throwing a warning glance at Delilah, said. "The weather is beautiful now, is it not? But such fog yesterday. Filthy stuff. All the curtains will need to be taken down and washed."

All the ladies, except Delilah, began to talk about the fog. Delilah felt miserable. She knew she had made a dreadful social gaffe in mentioning Mrs. Tomlinson's pregnancy.

"Lord Andrew Bergrave," announced the marchioness's butler. The gentleman who entered the room was not precisely handsome. But he was well-tailored, slim, and had a clever face and a pair of merry brown eyes. Those eyes lit on Delilah and he promptly demanded an introduction.

He pulled a chair up next to Delilah's and said, "Now you must just have arrived in Town, Miss Wraxall, otherwise I would have heard all talk of your beauty."

Effy, watching closely, noticed the caressing smile Delilah gave him and how she prettily raised her fan to her face as if to cover her confusion.

"You tease me, my lord," said Delilah. "There must be a great number of very beautiful ladies in London."

"None as beautiful as you, I swear," said Lord Andrew. "Do you plan to stay in Town for long?"

"I do not know, my lord," said Delilah. "I am staying with Miss Effy and Miss Amy Tribble."

A slight look of shock registered in Lord Andrew's eyes. "They are old friends of my father," added Delilah.

"Well, of course they are," he said with a little laugh. "Someone as perfect as you could hardly—"

He broke off and said instead, "You must allow me to take you driving in the Park, Miss Wraxall."

"I should like that above all things," said Delilah, giving him a blinding smile.

"And how is your mother, Lord Andrew?" interrupted the marchioness.

"Very well, ma'am. She sends her regards."

"The duchess must be relieved to have you back from the wars safe and sound. I remember staying with her on a visit when you were a very young man, Lord Andrew. But you had a superb pair of legs even then."

"You flatter me," said Lord Andrew.

"Not at all," said the marchioness. "I, too, have still a good leg. What are your legs like, Miss Effy?"

"Fair, I think," said Effy.

"Let us all show our legs!" cried the marchioness.

She hitched up her skirts, revealing thick legs like posts and a pair of scarlet garters. Miss Effy had quite a shapely pair, Mrs. Busby had a powerful pair of muscular ones, and Mrs. Tomlinson had varicose veins.

"Am I not to have the delight of seeing yours, Miss Wraxall?" asked Lord Andrew.

"Certainly not," said Delilah. She was deeply shocked. Effy then announced she was taking her leave. Lord Andrew whispered to Delilah that he would call as soon as possible.

As soon as they were seated in the carriage, Delilah burst out, "What odd behaviour! What peculiar standards! I ask that Mrs. Tomlinson about her baby and everyone looks as shocked as if I had mouthed an obscenity. And yet they all start to show their legs, exactly like a group of demi-reps."

"There are some things you must not do or say," said Effy. "You must never mention that a lady is with child. It is different in the country, where you have people and farm animals breeding in such an undisciplined way. But here in Town, it is considered vulgar to remark on a lady's condition. The marchioness is very good ton and therefore can be allowed a few eccentricities like showing her legs. You, Miss Wraxall, on the other hand, must behave with modesty at all times. Now, I noticed you flirting with Lord Andrew. You must be careful not to appear too forward. You may have given him a disgust of you."

Delilah tossed her head. "He is to call to ask your permission to take me driving."

"Be warned," said Effy severely. "There are a great many rakey-hell gentlemen in London who think that when a lady flirts too openly, it means her morals are not of the purest."

"At least I do not go around showing my legs," said Delilah huffily.

"Now we make a few more calls," said Effy, and Delilah just stopped herself from groaning aloud.

There were to be no more eligible men that day. Delilah met only elderly gentlemen and various ladies, all of whom went on as if she were not in the room.

She thought she heard one lady, after looking at her in surprise, whisper, "Another of the Tribbles' difficult ones. I wonder what is up with *her.*" But the whisper was so faint, she thought she must have misheard it.

When they returned to Holles Street, it was to find the squire and Amy sharing the tea-tray in high good humour. Delilah took her father aside. "Take me with you when you leave, Papa," she whispered. "I do not think I like London."

"Give it a chance," said her father. "I shall call again in a month's time, and if you are still of the same mind, then I shall take you away." And with that, Delilah had to be content.

Sir Charles Digby arrived in town a few days later. Lord Andrew was just about to leave to go out for the day. "Charles!" he cried. "Are you come to stay?"

"If you'll have me."

"For as long as you want. You must excuse me. I am off to drive an angel around the Park, but I shall be back very soon."

"What angel is that?"

"I am not telling you," said Lord Andrew. "She is but lately come to Town and I mean to keep her to myself for as long as possible."

Sir Charles oversaw the unpacking of his trunks, changed, and decided to go out and walk to White's in St. James's and renew his membership of that famous club. The sun was shining and everything looked fresh and glittering. The striped blinds were still down in front of the house windows and buff canopies protected the goods in the shop windows from the sun's glare. The ladies were in their prettiest muslins and the men were even better-tailored than he had remembered.

He was strolling along Piccadilly when he met Mr. Peter Macdonald, an old friend from a Scottish regiment. They hailed each other with delight and Mr. Macdonald fell into step beside him, saying he would go to the club as well. "And what brings you to Town?" asked Mr. Macdonald.

"I plan to enjoy myself," said Sir Charles. "My time is my own. I have only one duty to perform. Have you heard of a couple of ladies called Tribble?"

Mr. Macdonald laughed. "I have only been in Town a month, but I heard about them almost as soon as I arrived. A great pair of quizzes."

"In what way?"

"They are very good ton, but had fallen on hard times. So they began to advertise their services. That is, they swear they can take any difficult and unmarriageable miss and reform her. They have had two notable successes and the latest rumor is that they have just started off with a new charge."

"And where are they to be found?"

"Holles Street."

Sir Charles changed the conversation and began to talk of the war. They spent a pleasant time in White's, fighting old battles, and the matter of the Tribbles was forgotten.

Sir Charles finally returned to Brook Street to find that Lord Andrew had left again, leaving a note to say he had gone to dinner and would be back late, but Sir Charles was to summon the chef and order anything he wanted.

Sir Charles thought of the Tribbles again. They seemed an odd couple of friends for the squire to have. But he had promised Mrs. Cavendish to learn about this Miss Amy. He had an early dinner and decided to go to Holles Street and find out for himself.

Effy was sitting in the drawing-room, sewing, while Delilah inexpertly murdered a piece of Mozart on the piano. Delilah's playing was not normally so bad. She was puzzling over in her mind various things Lord Andrew had said that afternoon. He would start to ask her why she had been sent to the Tribbles and then hurriedly say it did not matter. Again she had said the Tribbles were old friends of her father.

The butler entered and handed Effy a card. "Don't know him," said Effy. "Tell him we are not at home."

"He says he's a friend of Mr. Wraxall," said Harris.

"Oh, in that case, you'd best send him up," sighed Effy. "I do wish Amy would stop jauntering about to every unfashionable place in Town." She raised her voice. "Do stop playing, Miss Wraxall. We have company."

Delilah swung round on the piano stool. She glanced at the clock. "Does one usually receive callers in London at eight in the evening?"

"No," said Effy, "but this is some friend of your father's."

Delilah's face lit up. It would be nice to see someone from the village.

"Sir Charles Digby," announced Harris.

"Oh, lor'," said Effy, suddenly remembering the name of the man who had broken Delilah's heart. Delilah's face was quite stiff and set.

Sir Charles was staring at her as if he could not believe his eyes.

"What are you doing here, Miss Wraxall?" he exclaimed.

Effy coughed gently and Sir Charles swung to face her. "My apologies," he said. "Do I have the honour of meeting Miss Amy Tribble?"

"No, sir, I am her sister, Miss Effy Tribble. Pray be seated, Sir Charles. Mr. Wraxall is an old friend, and my sister and I decided it would be a good idea to give Miss Wraxall some time in London."

"You did not tell me you were travelling to Town, Miss Wraxall," said Sir Charles.

"Neither did you," pointed out Delilah. "So why did you decide to call here?"

"Mrs. Cavendish told me that the Misses Tribble were friends of your father and I thought it only polite to call and pay my respects."

"And does my father know of your plans to call?" asked Delilah.

"No, I did not have time to speak to him."

"He is here, in Town," said Delilah, "but plans to leave tomorrow. He is at the moment attending a performance at Astley's Amphitheatre with Miss Amy."

"Tell him I am sorry to miss him."

"How can you be sorry when you did not expect to see either me or him in the first place?" pointed out Delilah rudely.

"If this is an example of your social manners, Miss Wraxall, then I am not surprised your father decided to ask for expert help."

"What are you talking about?"

Effy flashed Sir Charles a warning look. So, thought Sir Charles, Delilah *had* been sent away to be schooled. What was up with her? There *must* be something up with her or she would be married.

Effy glanced from one to the other. Delilah looked magnificent with her eyes flashing fire. Sir Charles with his lean, athletic body, tanned face, black eyes and fair hair was quite devastatingly handsome. Effy sighed. What a pair of heart-breakers they were.

"I was merely pointing out that you are rude, Miss Wraxall."

"I fear the war has made you unfit for the drawing-room, sir," said Delilah, "for it is very rude of *you* to remark on my behaviour."

"If you are come to Town in the hopes of finding a husband, then that hoydenish manner of yours is going to bring you nothing but failure," said Sir Charles.

Delilah suddenly smiled at him. "Oh, my poor Sir Charles," she said softly. "How blind you are. I can be married at any time I like and to anyone who pleases me."

"Not to me," said Sir Charles.

"Of course not," said Delilah sweetly. "For you do not please me in the slightest!"

Sir Charles got to his feet. "I wish you the joy of Miss Wraxall's education," he said to Effy. "You are going to have a great deal of work."

"How could you be so horrible, Delilah?" exclaimed Effy when Sir Charles had left.

"Pooh!" said Delilah and turned about and started battering the piano again.

Sir Charles did not see his friend until breakfast the following day. "How was your dinner party?" he asked.

Lord Andrew rubbed his bloodshot eyes. "Famous, what I remember of it," he said. "I was telling one of my best stories and suddenly I found myself lying under the table with not the slightest idea of how I got there. My head! My days of racketing around are at an end. Time to get married and settle down."

"And have you anyone in mind?"

"A divine creature from your part of the world. If I tell

you her name, will you give me your sincere promise not
to try to cut me out?"

"I promise."

"Miss Delilah Wraxall."

"I know her well. Her father is the squire of Hoppleton.
As a matter of fact, I got the shock of my life when I found
her resident with those Tribbles."

"Because they advertise for difficult girls? That is not
the case with Miss Wraxall. The Tribbles are old friends
of her father and she is in no need of schooling. Such
divine looks, such grace, such charm of manner!"

"You are fortunate. I appear to bring out the beast in
Miss Wraxall. She was most rude to me."

"Good," said Lord Andrew heartlessly. "High time you
had a set-down. You are a sad philanderer."

"I? My dear Andrew. When did I ever play fast and
loose with any woman's affections?"

"Before Salamanca. That captain's widow, you know,
pretty little thing. Cried her eyes out when you wouldn't
look at her again. Swore you'd made love to her."

"I may have flirted a little, but she did encourage me,
and it was that rare party when we were all having as
much fun as we could in case we died the next day."

"Mrs. Agnew, that was her name," said Lord Andrew.
"You were cuddling her. I saw you."

"You weren't exactly behaving like a saint yourself, as
I recall," said Sir Charles.

"Ah, but I was paying assiduous court to that hardened
flirt, Jessica Bond-Fallen. No heart to break there, nor
reputation to lose, either."

"Well, I am sorry. I did not expect her to take me
seriously."

"A rich, handsome, marriageable man is always taken
seriously."

Sir Charles fell silent. He remembered kissing Delilah and how the squire had asked him if he had encouraged her in any way. But Delilah could not, surely, have taken him seriously; or, if by any chance she had, then she was too beautiful a creature to remain pining for any man for long. But why had she never married?

"Is she rich as well as beautiful?" asked Lord Andrew.

"Yes, Miss Wraxall is very rich. How so? You are not short of a shilling."

"Been dipping deep," said Lord Andrew. "Do not follow my example. Keep away from the gaming tables of St. James's."

"I have no intention of playing," said Sir Charles. "I have no desire to lose my estates."

London was in the grip of ferocious gambling fever. At those famous clubs, White's, Boodle's, and Brooks's in St. James's Street, it was nothing for a gentleman to lose thirty thousand or forty thousand pounds in a single evening. Raggett, the proprietor of White's, used to sit up with the gamblers all through the night, sending his servants to bed, so that he could sweep the carpets himself in the early hours of the morning to retrieve the gold carelessly scattered on the floor.

Very few of the noble gentlemen who played ever emerged into the street as winners. The one notable exception was the Duke of Portland's father-in-law, General Scott, who dined simply off boiled chicken, toast and water to keep a clear head and cool judgement at the whist table. In this way, he succeeded in winning the enormous sum of two hundred thousand pounds. It appeared as if the great aristocratic families who had inherited the accumulated wealth of the eighteenth century were hell-bent on squandering the lot in the pleasure-loving days of the Regency.

"I trust," said Sir Charles, "you are not thinking of marrying Miss Wraxall solely because of her wealth."

"No, by Gad! Worship the ground she walks on, I assure you. Still, I never did believe in love in a cottage and I would dearly like a wife who would keep me happy by paying for my customary pleasures."

Sir Charles fought down a sudden stab of dislike for his friend. Still, if Delilah was the minx she was reputed to be, then she might lead Lord Andrew a merry dance.

Chapter 4

Now, don't look so glum and sanctified, please,
For folks, comme il faut, *sir, are always at*
ease; How dare you suggest that my talk is too
free? Il n'est jamais de mal en bon
compagnie.

Charles Brooks

DELILAH HAD LED QUITE A busy life in the country. Although there were balls and parties, most of the time was taken up with sewing clothes for the poor, visiting the sick, making jams and cordials, gardening, reading, painting, and many other activities.

It was not that she was idle in London. It simply struck her as rather odd that society should boast of being idle and yet spend so much work and energy on their amusements. Lessons by the music tutor were followed by lessons by a French teacher, then an Italian teacher, and then came a dancing master to show her the steps of the quadrille.

65

All this activity did have the merit of making the days pass quickly.

She had taken affectionate leave of her father, who had again promised solemnly to return in a month's time and, if she were unhappy, to take her home.

Delilah did not expect Sir Charles to call again, nor would she admit to herself that, when Lord Andrew told her Sir Charles was staying in London at his house, she had proceeded to encourage the attentions of that young man more than she ought.

But she could not help wondering whether Sir Charles meant to attend the ball at Lady Burgoyne's. She wanted him to see how fêted she was, how popular with the gentlemen. Even after all those years, it was important to Delilah that Sir Charles should believe that that farewell kiss had meant nothing to her.

In all, Delilah felt she had enough to do to make the time until her father's return pass quickly.

Had it not been for a nagging worry that her father meant to propose to Miss Amy Tribble, Delilah would have been quite happy.

Amy wandered about in a dream from which Effy's occasional sharp remarks failed to rouse her. She was remembering and savouring her last talk with the squire.

They had had a splendid time at Astley's, cheering the equestrians and crying at the sentimental plays. The squire had called the next day to take his leave of Delilah and then had requested a few moments alone with Miss Amy.

He had pressed her hand warmly. He had said, "I never hoped to be comfortable in the company of a lady after my wife died, Miss Amy. Now, you have changed all that. As soon as Delilah is settled, I must consider my own future. I had not thought to marry again, but . . ." His voice had trailed off and he had not said any more, but it was enough for Amy. Her only regret was that Mr. Haddon was not in London. She hoped he would be back in time to hear of her engagement. Effy could have him. Mr. Haddon should learn that he had let a desirable lady escape.

And then on the afternoon before Lady Burgoyne's ball, a row erupted which roused even Amy from her dreams.

Delilah had gone out with Effy to make calls. At Mrs. Busby's, Delilah had met a young miss called Mary Williams who, like Delilah, was in London for the first time. Mrs. Busby was her aunt. While their elders were talking, Delilah and Mary shared their first impressions of London. Mary confided in Delilah her hopes of being engaged soon so as to spare her parents the expense of a full Season.

"I am sure *you* will not have any worries," said Mary. "The Misses Tribble are accounted very successful at puffing girls off."

"Indeed!" exclaimed Delilah. "Do they have nieces they have brought out?"

"No, just the people they advertise for. I assume your papa read their advertisement."

"What advertisement?" asked Delilah.

It was then obvious to Mary that Delilah knew very little about the Tribbles. But she was jealous of Delilah's glowing beauty and said, "They advertise for difficult girls, you know, girls whose parents cannot do anything to get them wed. I know this cannot be true in your case, dear Miss Wraxall, but it must make you feel very odd, everyone wondering what is up with you."

"The Misses Tribble are old friends of my father, that is all," said Delilah coldly.

Mary moved away to talk to someone else. Delilah thought furiously. She thought of all the tutors, the constant admonitions as to how to behave, Lord Andrew's odd remarks. She could feel her face beginning to burn. As soon as they returned to Holles Street, Delilah faced the sisters. Some instinct told her that if she asked them whether her father had answered their advertisement, then they might stick to the fiction that he was simply an old friend. Instead she lied. "My father informs me he is paying you to school me," she said.

Amy looked startled, and then said, "Well, he might have told us he had told you. He instructed us to say we were old friends of his."

"So it *is* true!" raged Delilah. "Why? I have had more proposals of marriage than most women in England."

Effy twittered in dismay, but Amy said roundly, "You didn't accept any of 'em. What worries your father is that you led them all on shamelessly, or they would never have come up to the mark. He turned to us because he was at his wits' end."

"Why didn't he tell me?" cried Delilah.

"Probably thought you wouldn't listen," said Amy. "He says you never got over that Sir Charles Digby turning you down. Took your revenge on everyone else."

"Sir Charles Digby means nothing to me, never did," said Delilah. "I shall leave this day."

"You will not leave," said Amy, who now viewed herself as Delilah's stepmother. "It is high time you started thinking of other people. Yes! What of your father? How can he get married again with you hanging around his neck?"

"Meaning you hope he will marry you," said Delilah.

Amy threw back her head. "Yes," she said defiantly. "He has more or less declared himself."

"Oh, poor, poor Amy," sighed Effy. "How your wishful thinking does mislead you so."

"Bitch and hell-cat," raged Amy. "How can you know anything about love, Effy, you with your chin-straps and face creams and with that embroidered pincushion you call a brain?"

"Listen to both of you," jeered Delilah. *"You* are supposed to tell *me* how to go on? You have the manners of the gutter, Miss Amy."

"And you have the manners of a slut," shouted Amy.

"I am going to write to my father now," said Delilah, "and I am going to ask him to come to London immediately and take me away."

She swept from the room.

The sisters looked at each other in dismay. Amy sat down and tugged at her hair.

"We handled that very badly," said Effy quietly. "We cannot afford to lose Delilah. It seemed like a miracle to have work for the Little Season and not to have to wait until the real Season begins."

"We'll manage," said Amy gruffly.

"You are overset because for some reason you expect the squire to propose marriage," said Effy. "He will not, Amy. Oh, I know he likes you, but there is nothing of the lover there."

Amy looked up. "It's no use hoping it ain't true, Effy. He said I made him think of marriage."

Effy began to cry. "What will I do?" she cried. "I shall be left here on my own to manage savage girls."

"Now, now," said Amy. "Don't cry. You can come and live with us."

"But the country!" wailed Effy. "I hate the country. Oh, are you really sure of this, Amy? What of Mr. Haddon?"

"Mr. Haddon is fond of both of us, Effy. But face facts.

He's an old stick of a bachelor and will always be that way."

Delilah penned a letter to her father and then instructed Harris to have it sent express. Then, when her fury died down, it was replaced by a recurrence of the miserable thought that all her flirting and romancing had been discussed and worried over behind her back. It seemed to Delilah as if the whole of Kent was discussing her humiliation at the hands of Sir Charles and assuming she had turned down so many because she could not have him.

She now hated Sir Charles. He had walked back into her life—calm, handsome and indifferent. She was stranded in this odd house with these odd sisters, one of whom was about to become her stepmother. There was no going back to her old life.

Baxter came in and began to lay out Delilah's gown for the ball. Delilah looked at her in surprise. She had assumed, after all the shocks and revelations, that she would not be going and neither would the Tribbles.

But she felt too upset to face any more rows by declaring she was staying at home. In a stony silence, she allowed Baxter to dress her and fix her hair.

She went down to the drawing-room to join Amy and Effy, her face set in hard, haughty lines.

Delilah was nearly bowled over by Amy, who rushed forward and clasped her in her arms. "I am a boor and a beast," said Amy. "Please say you forgive me, Miss Wraxall."

"Yes, do forgive us," said Effy quietly as Amy released Delilah and stood back. "It must have come as a shock to you to learn your father was paying for our services. We quite understand your wish to leave. But do consider, we can have a little fun and perhaps enjoy ourselves."

"You must need my father's money very badly," said Delilah.

"Oh, yes," said Amy seriously. "It is very hard to have to work for one's money. One is so at the mercy of people's whims."

Delilah looked at the odd pair of sisters: Effy, so delicate and pretty, Amy, so tall and masculine. "Tell me," she asked curiously, "how did you plan to . . . er . . . reform me?"

Amy thought quickly. They had not, in fact, had any plan of campaign, merely hoping to refine Delilah's behaviour as they went along. But she said slowly, "I think, you know, we would have encouraged Sir Charles to call here as often as possible and may even have held a dinner in his honour."

"Why?" exclaimed Delilah.

Amy wrinkled her brow. "You see, you were seventeen the time he left for the wars. Your papa told me you were pretty then but hardly as beautiful or modish as you are now. Sir Charles was twenty-eight then and a mature man worrying about going to the wars. He is now thirty-four and you are twenty-three, so there is less of an emotional age difference between the two of you. I think, you know, you would find it very easy indeed to make Sir Charles Digby fall in love with you. Then *you* could spurn *him* and perhaps that would change your mind and encourage you to settle down."

"I do not know why everyone insists on damning me as a heart-breaker," said Delilah. "Sir Charles means nothing to me."

But Amy's words about making Sir Charles fall in love with her were like balm to Delilah's angry soul.

"In any case," put in Effy, "it will be a most unpleasant house to live in if we are all at loggerheads. Do forgive us, Miss Wraxall."

"Of course I do," said Delilah. "You were only following my father's instructions. I shall take the matter up with him when I see him. But why am *I* damned as so bad? Plenty of women flirt; it is the fashion."

"Flirting is an art in itself and forgivable in most," said Amy. "But beautiful people should not flirt. You see, they don't need to. Their beauty is enough. If they add flirting to it, then they break hearts. Everyone knows when a plain girl is flirting, but every man thinks a beauty must surely be in love with him. Wishful thinking is a pernicious thing."

"As you should know," muttered Effy, but Amy ignored her and cast an expert eye over Delilah's appearance.

Delilah was wearing a white muslin gown edged with gold embroidery. Pearls threaded on gold chain were wound among her black curls. Her hazel eyes were very large and flecked with green and gold under thick black curling lashes.

As they set out for the ball, the spirits of all three began to rise. Now that Delilah knew the real reason for her visit to London, it did not seem so very bad. It had been hard to remain angry when these odd ladies had begged her forgiveness. She was looking forward now to meeting the challenge of demonstrating to London society that there was nothing up with her at all. And as far as London society knew, the Tribbles really were friends of her father. It was not the main Season, and so that added credence to the lie.

Effy and Amy were looking forward to the sensation Delilah must surely make at the ball. Amy was dreaming of how life would be after she married the squire. No more worries and frights about money, no more waiting each morning for the post, hoping for a new client, a new difficult girl to ensure them security for another year. Perhaps, thought Amy, she and Effy might save money by taking lessons from all these tutors themselves. That way they could train their charges themselves in French and Italian, music and painting.

Effy was hoping that there might be some gentleman at the ball who would fall in love with her. Effy's bright hopes had remained undiminished down the years. She had only to put one little foot on some red-carpeted staircase leading to a ballroom and hear the sound of the fiddles for her heart to rise, for a suffocating excitement to grip her throat. *He* might be there, that dream gentleman might be waiting there, to become reality.

London was coming to life for the night ahead. It had its own particular night-time smell, a mixture of patchouli, whale oil, bad drains, pomatum and hot hair from all the tresses that were being frizzled by the curling tongs in hundreds of rooms.

There was never very far to travel anywhere in the West End of London, but to arrive on foot was a social disgrace, and to arrive in a hack, something worse. So they waited patiently as their carriage inched forward through the press, stopping and starting. Delilah was reminded of that first journey through the fog.

At last they were able to alight in front of a tall double-fronted mansion with liveried footmen holding torches lining the steps. A red carpet was stretched out over the pavement in front of the house, a heady luxury. Behind the flares of the torches stood a crowd of people, waiting to see the rich and great arrive.

Delilah caught a glimpse of them as she walked up towards the house and wondered what they thought and whether they were ever angry at the sheer unfairness of life where just one of these guests' jewels could keep a London family in comfort for quite a long time. Delilah, like everyone else, knew that the churches said that men and women were placed by God in their appointed stations, and to cry out against such a state of affairs was ungodly. But she could not help thinking that if she were one of those unfortunates, she would be very tempted to turn to a life of crime to even the score.

Standing in the ballroom with Lord Andrew, Sir Charles saw Delilah arrive. He had expected her to be outshone by all the London belles, but all about him he heard exclamations at her beauty. "I had better move fast," muttered Lord Andrew. "My heiress will slip through my fingers if I am not careful."

He hurried to Delilah's side. Sir Charles frowned. He had promised his friend not to interfere in his pursuit of the girl, but, on the other hand, surely his loyalty to Delilah and her father came first. It would do no harm to warn Delilah against fortune-hunters in general. Someone else came up to talk to him and kept him quite ten minutes so that by the time he looked up again, Delilah had taken the floor.

Amy and Effy noticed Sir Charles watching Delilah and put their heads together. "I swear he is not indifferent to her," said Amy. "I think it would be easy for Delilah to get her revenge if she wished. Here he comes. I think he wants to speak to us."

"How handsome he is," sighed Effy. "Do but look at his legs, Amy."

Sir Charles bowed before them. Both sisters rose and curtsied and then all three sat down together. "Miss Wraxall is a sensation," said Amy.

"I suppose I am too late now to have the pleasure of a dance with her," said Sir Charles.

"I should think so," said Effy. "But she is just beginning to learn the steps of the quadrille. I do not think she will try to dance it this evening, so if you were to approach her when it is announced, you may be able to sit out with her."

"I shall do that," said Sir Charles. Delilah was dancing with Lord Andrew. She had been determined not to flirt, but old habits die hard, and as Sir Charles looked, Delilah gave Lord Andrew a definitely flirtatious glance.

"Is it generally known that Miss Wraxall is rich?" asked Sir Charles.

"Not yet," said Amy. "But it will be. A lady who is known to have a large dowry can quickly have her choice of suitors."

Sir Charles surveyed the sisters in some irritation. "Would it not have been better to have kept such a fact quiet?" he demanded. "Miss Wraxall is beautiful enough to attract many men without having to fend off fortune-hunters."

"Lord Andrew is hardly a fortune-hunter," exclaimed Effy.

"Any man who gambles is a fortune-hunter these days," said Sir Charles. "Ladies are at a disadvantage. Now, men can see the betting books in the clubs and know who has lost a fortune and who has gained one. Take the Honourable Freddy Ribble over there. He is accounted rich, is he not?"

"Yes, an eligible," said Amy, who kept a book of what she called "the runners" at home.

"He lost thirty-five thousand pounds at Watier's playing macao last night."

"Good heavens," said Amy. "Who won?"

"The money was won by Lord Freemount, who is not only sixty and a lecher but who is like to lose the whole amount this very evening. He is a true gambler, which means he cannot rest until he has lost it all again."

"What a useful source of information you are!" exclaimed Effy. "It is most unfair that you should not only be handsome but intelligent as well." She rolled her eyes up at him and rapped him playfully with her fan.

"Such delicacy and beauty as yours, ma'am, must surely inspire any man," said Sir Charles dutifully.

Effy let out a trill of laughter and hid her imaginary blushes behind her fan.

"Really, Effy," said Amy crossly. "How are we to stop Delilah flirting if you set such a bad example?"

"Is that your aim?" asked Sir Charles. "To stop Delilah flirting?"

"It's not that Miss Wraxall is precisely a flirt," said Amy. "It is just that with her looks and money she does not need to encourage anyone."

"Squire Wraxall should never have brought her to London," said Sir Charles. "There are men a-plenty in Kent."

"But I gather she has turned down practically every eligible man in that county," said Amy. "Perhaps she needs gentlemen who are more worldly-wise and fashionable."

"We are not all yokels and bumpkins in the country," said Sir Charles.

"But perhaps you lack a certain finesse," said Effy slyly. "No one in London society leads any lady to suppose their intentions are serious unless they themselves are serious."

"That is nonsense."

"It is true. Gentlemen flirt outrageously with the fast matrons and the demi-reps. The Fribbles pay court to the latest belle, but even she knows not to take their attentions seriously. A London gentleman, for example, would never kiss a lady unless he had obtained permission first from parents or guardians to pay his addresses."

Effy thought she was being very subtle and clever, but it told Sir Charles in plain words that the Tribbles had learned he had kissed Delilah. With a sinking heart, he realized he had behaved thoughtlessly and carelessly to a young girl. Delilah was now a beautiful woman and much desired. He hoped she had forgotten that episode but decided it would be better if he apologized for it in case she had not.

He took his leave of the Tribbles and went off and danced a few reels and waltzes until he heard the quadrille being announced. Delilah, who had been promenading after the last dance with her partner, as was the custom, looked up as he approached.

Her partner bowed and left. "Do you dance the quadrille?" asked Sir Charles.

"Not yet," said Delilah. "It is a very hard dance. My dancing master tells me that the ladies who perform it are expected to do entrechats, but every time I try them, I fall on the floor."

"Then let us have some refreshment," he said, guiding her towards the room set apart for the guests to eat and drink.

They found a table in the supper room. Delilah said she would like champagne, as lemonade seemed too ordinary a drink for London.

She was feeling elated with her success. She was also feeling elated by the fact that here was Sir Charles Digby sitting quite close to her and it didn't mean a thing.

"Are you enjoying London?" he asked.

"I am beginning to," said Delilah, "but so many lessons! It seems a great waste of effort to learn French and Italian so that one can interlard one's conversation with a great many foreign phrases. I prefer to converse in plain English."

"I, too," said Sir Charles. "But it is the fashion. Soon, you will have to learn to lisp as well."

"God forbid!"

"Oh, but any fashionable miss must learn to speak like a two-year-old."

"What a great deal of work it takes for a woman to appear useless, stupid, and idle," said Delilah.

"I am glad of this opportunity to talk to you, Miss Wraxall," said Sir Charles. "You know I am residing with Lord Andrew?"

"Yes." Delilah's face brightened. "Such a kind and amusing man."

"There are many kind and amusing men in London. You must, however, be on your guard against fortune-hunters. Quite a number of gentlemen from the oldest and noblest families in England have become adventurers because they have lost their fortunes on the gaming tables and might look to your dowry to restore those fortunes."

"I am no longer a silly little girl whose head is easily turned," said Delilah.

Sir Charles studied her. "I owe you an apology," he said abruptly.

Delilah continued to sip champagne but did not reply.

"Before I went off to the wars," said Sir Charles, "you may remember that I kissed you."

Delilah wrinkled her brow. "Did you?" she asked.

He felt himself becoming very angry. "I kissed you because I was leaving home and did not think I would come back."

"Dear me," said Delilah lightly. "What a peculiar way to go about it. More sensible to have kissed the bricks of your house."

"You are deliberately misunderstanding me."

"Not I," said Delilah, her beautiful eyes roaming about the room as if already seeking more entertaining company.

"In any case," said Sir Charles, "I beg you to accept my apology."

"Well . . . well . . . ," said Delilah, stifling a yawn. "If it means so much to you, then I accept your apology. Although it is very hard to accept an apology for an action one has totally forgotten. Oh, here is Lord Andrew!" she cried with obvious relief. "Lord Andrew, are you come to rescue me?"

"The next dance is a waltz and promised to me," said Lord Andrew.

"Two dances, my lord," said Delilah, rising to her feet. "How people will talk!"

"They will indeed," said Lord Andrew. "All the fellows will be cursing me for a lucky dog. Lady, I would it were an hundred dances. I would dance with you for the rest of my life."

"How terribly fatiguing," said Delilah with a ripple of laughter. She moved off with Lord Andrew, leaving Sir Charles alone.

Sir Charles was furious with Delilah. He had tried to warn her against fortune-hunters, he had tried to apologize for that kiss, and all he had done was to bore her.

He did not like the way she was behaving. Surely he owed it to the squire to make sure his daughter would not throw away her fortune on Lord Andrew.

Delilah danced and danced and Sir Charles did not approach her again. She wished he would, for she felt she had not yet proved how indifferent she was to him. As she was leaving, Lord Andrew came up to her and said he had made up a party of young people to go over to the Surrey fields for a picnic on the morrow if the weather stayed fine, and that the Tribbles had given him permission to take her. The Tribbles had noticed how annoyed Lord Andrew's attentions seemed to be making Sir Charles and had decided to irritate that gentleman further. So while Lord Andrew was talking to Delilah, Amy went up to Sir Charles and said, "I hope we have done the right thing. Lord Andrew is to take Miss Wraxall on a picnic on the morrow. A party of young people, you know. Let me see, there is young Lady Devere, Mr. Tommy Otterley, Miss Pretty-Follip, and Lord Henry. As far as I know, they are all very respectable."

"Do you consider Lord Andrew a suitable beau?" asked Sir Charles abruptly.

"Perhaps," said Amy. "I must confess I wish now I had not given my permission. I would dearly like to suggest you go along yourself, Sir Charles, just to keep an eye on Miss Wraxall. You are so much older than she. I am sure she looks on you as a sort of uncle, you being from the same village."

Sir Charles was about to say haughtily that he had no intention of wasting an afternoon chaperoning Delilah, but then he thought again he owed it to the people of the village and to Squire Wraxall to make sure that Delilah did not form a mésalliance.

"Perhaps I shall go," he said. "At what time does this outing take place?"

"They are to call for Miss Wraxall at two in the afternoon."

"Then I shall be there."

Amy watched him go with satisfaction. Instead of encouraging Delilah to get her revenge on Sir Charles, perhaps it would be better to encourage her to marry him. Amy still saw herself in the light of Delilah's future stepmother. Sir Charles's land bordered that of the squire's. It would be an eminently suitable marriage and two such very handsome people surely belonged together.

She thought of the squire and a warm glow spread

slowly through her flat-chested bosom. Perhaps he might arrive again before the month was up. Perhaps he might even write. What had he been doing this evening while they were at the ball? Probably sitting at home by the firelight, alone.

The squire, feeling oddly shy and nervous, had put on his best clothes and gone calling on Mrs. Cavendish.

He was amazed at the difference in his home since Delilah had left. Nothing seemed quite as pretty or comfortable. There were no flower arrangements to decorate the rooms, no comfortable conversations in the evening, no life or movement about the house.

Everything in Mrs. Cavendish's little cottage appeared warm and cosy. The fire blazed in the hearth and the air was scented from the bowls of pot-pourri placed about the room.

The squire sighed and stretched his feet out to the blaze. He thought fondly of Miss Amy Tribble, who had taken away a lot of his shyness and fear of women. Earlier that evening, he had felt that shyness return, but now he was here, he knew it was going to be all right. He looked affectionately at Mrs. Cavendish's round and pleasant face and felt at home.

Mrs. Cavendish bustled about, serving tea, and sending up prayers that no one else would call.

They then talked in their usual way about the gossip of the village.

"And how is Delilah?" asked Mrs. Cavendish at last. "I suppose it's too early yet for you to have received a letter."

"Yes, but I feel a great responsibility has been taken off

my shoulders," said Mr. Wraxall. "How competent and wise Miss Amy is, Mrs. Cavendish."

"So you have said many, many times," said Mrs. Cavendish. "More cake?"

"Yes, I thank you. I must confess I was worried when I learned that Sir Charles, too, is in London, but it's a big place. Perhaps they will not meet."

Mrs. Cavendish felt guilty. She had received a letter from Sir Charles only that day in which he had said that the Tribble sisters were a trifle eccentric, but good ton. Unfortunately, he had not described Miss Amy. He wrote that they had a reputation for schooling awkward ladies and could no doubt be trusted to do their best with Delilah. He added he was sure Delilah would be soon wed as her beauty was exceptional, even set against such beauties as there were in London.

It had been, reflected Mrs. Cavendish, a depressing letter, depressing in that it heralded a squire soon to be free of the cares of parenthood. It also meant that Mrs. Cavendish was somehow going to have to tell the squire she had sent Sir Charles to spy out the land. And what reason could she possibly give?

To say she was not sure of the Tribbles would be to question the squire's judgement. To say she hoped to bring Sir Charles and Delilah together looked like interference. The very truth that she was wildly jealous of Miss Amy Tribble could not be said.

"It is a pity about Sir Charles and Miss Wraxall," she said. "I always thought them very much suited."

"He was too old for her then," sighed the squire. "He is not now. You know how it is. The older one gets, the less the age difference."

They fell silent. Mrs. Cavendish decided she really must say something about having sent Sir Charles to the

Tribbles. The words trembled on her lips. She leaned forward.

"I have something to say to you, Mrs. Cavendish," said the squire, putting down his cup. "Something very serious . . . very important."

He has found out about Sir Charles's going to the Tribbles, thought Mrs. Cavendish.

"It is about Miss Amy Tribble," said the squire and Mrs. Cavendish reflected dismally that she would rather it *had* been about her sending Sir Charles.

"Since my wife died," said Sir Charles, "I have become awkward and shy in the company of women. I married, as you know, when I was just eighteen. My wife, Lucinda, was very frail, and we thought we would not have any children until, after some years, we were blessed with Delilah. I do not know, had she lived, if my dear wife would have known how to cope with Delilah. She was timid, retiring, and always ill. After her death, I found myself more at ease in the company of men. That was, until I met Miss Amy."

Damn her, thought Mrs. Cavendish, and blinked her eyes rapidly and prayed she would not cry.

"She is so straightforward, so easy to get along with. We talked for hours and hours. She brought me to the realization that there was one lady in my life I could marry, one lady I felt at home with, one lady I loved."

Now I *am* going to cry, thought poor Mrs. Cavendish, fighting with the hard lump which had risen in her throat.

The squire rose and got down on one knee in front of her.

"You are that lady, Mrs. Cavendish. Will you marry me?"

Mrs. Cavendish turned quite white. It was a heady rush up from hell to heaven all in one moment.

"Yes," she said. "Oh, yes. Yes, I will, Simon. Oh, yes, please."

He rose and leaned over her chair and kissed her very gently on the lips. "I shall send an express tomorrow and tell Delilah our good news," he said.

The party of young people set out next day. Sir Charles was regretting his decision to go and had prayed for rain, but the Indian summer had returned and the streets of London were bathed in gold light and the weather was warm and balmy.

He disapproved of Delilah's pale-green muslin gown and pelisse. It was cut in wickedly simple lines and made her figure more seductive and her eyes green. She was driving in an open carriage ahead of him with Lord Andrew. He himself was alone, since no one had expected him to come.

Although Lord Andrew was roughly the same age as he, the rest of the party were younger. He felt old and cross and grumpy listening to the gales of laughter coming from the other carriages.

He wished he had not come. He was not hungry and hated eating in the middle of the afternoon. He looked again at the sky. There was a milky veil covering the sun but no sign of rain.

It was unthinkable that such fashionable people should actually go to the effort of serving their own food, so there was a coachload of servants tagging along behind.

As soon as they arrived at a pleasant field, the ladies and gentlemen strolled about while the servants unpacked hampers and spread rugs and cushions on the grass. Sir Charles found he was taking care of Miss Pretty-Follip and Lady Devere. Mr. Tommy Otterley, Lord Henry and

Lord Andrew were all clustered about Delilah, hanging on her every word.

Delilah had forgotten her resolution to behave correctly. It was important that Sir Charles should see how popular she was, how desired. She teased and flirted, walking with first one and then another, seeming at one moment to favour Lord Andrew and then, the next instance, one of the other two gentlemen.

They were just sitting down to their picnic when there came a threatening rumble of thunder. Sir Charles looked up in surprise at the massed purple and black thunderclouds which were rapidly covering the sun. His prayers were about to be answered.

There were squeals of dismay. Lord Andrew suggested they move to a nearby posting-house and take their refreshment there. Off they went while the servants were left to pack everything up again.

Sir Charles tried to point out that the posting-house was not a good idea. If they delayed their journey, then they might get soaked on the road home. Everyone else seemed determined to go.

He followed the party, trying to think of a way to get his revenge on Delilah. He was sure her disgraceful flirtatious behaviour was for his benefit. When they reached the posting-house, however, there seemed to be little he could do. They were all seated around a large table in the coffee room. Lord Andrew was calling for champagne and cakes and the ladies were determinedly trying to outshine Delilah but without any success at all.

Sir Charles felt he could not bear these chattering, laughing idiots any more. He muttered an excuse and made his way through to the tap in order to have a little time to himself.

And then there at a table in the bay window, he saw

a group of young bloods playing dice. He stood for a few moments watching the play.

One of them finally stood up and pushed his chair back. "Care to take my place, sir?" he asked Sir Charles. "My pockets are to let."

"No," said Sir Charles. "But I think I know some gentlemen who would."

He strolled back to the coffee room. Lord Andrew was toasting Delilah's beauty, loudly echoed by Mr. Otterley and Lord Henry.

"There's a bunch of flats in the tap," Sir Charles said when he could make himself heard. "They are playing dice. Felt like showing them a thing or two."

Lord Andrew slowly lowered his glass. His eyes gleamed. "In the tap, you say? Might just have a look."

Mr. Otterley and Lord Henry exchanged glances. As Lord Andrew opened the door of the coffee room, they could clearly hear the seductive rattle of dice.

"Perhaps we had better just go after him and see he does not get into any trouble," said Mr. Otterley. He and Lord Henry left as well.

Sir Charles ignored Delilah's fulminating look and turned his attention to Miss Pretty-Follip and Lady Devere and proceeded to show Miss Delilah Wraxall a lesson in the art of flirtation. While Miss Pretty-Follip and Lady Devere wriggled and pouted and giggled, Delilah sat ignored by all.

There was a flash of lightning, followed by a terrific crash of thunder. The rain began to drum down outside.

"We are going to be trapped here for some time," said Sir Charles cheerfully.

"I am tired of all this," said Delilah. "I wish to go home."

"I do not have a closed carriage, so you will just need

to have patience and wait until the rain has stopped," said Sir Charles sweetly.

Delilah glared at him and walked out.

He waited, amused, for her return. But after a quarter of an hour had passed and there was no sign of her, he made his excuses to the two ladies and went to look for her, only to find that she had rented a closed carriage and left for London.

Miss Pretty-Follip and Lady Devere wondered what had happened to their gallant cavalier. A handsome, flirtatious man had left the room in search of Miss Wraxall, and an angry, stiff, and formal gentleman had returned. Sir Charles tried to console himself with the thought that he had done what he had set out to do. He was very sure that Delilah would not speak to Lord Andrew again.

He could now get down to the business of looking for a wife for himself. He thought the thundery weather must be affecting his spleen, he felt so low and bored at the very thought of wife-hunting.

Chapter 5

Say what you will, 'tis better to be left, than
never to have been loved.

William Congreve

ALTHOUGH EFFY WAS DIS-
MAYED when Delilah confessed
to having written an express to her father, demanding
that he come to Town and give her an immediate explanation as to why he had placed her with the Tribbles, Amy
was delighted. She would see the squire again. The sisters
had received a polite letter from Mr. Haddon saying he
expected to be back in London soon. Amy wanted to
secure her triumph before his return. It was only just that
Mr. Haddon should be brought to a speedy appreciation
of the prize that he had missed securing for himself.

Delilah continued her lessons on the pianoforte. She
was now a passable dancer of the quadrille. She begged

the Tribbles to dispense with the Italian and French tutors as she could not bring herself to follow the fashion by speaking in either of those languages. Delilah considered such a practice affected and would have none of it.

Amy dismissed the Italian teacher, but Effy insisted on retaining the French tutor, saying she wished to become fluent in that language herself. The French master, Monsieur Duclos, was quite attractive, a fact that the squire-besotted Amy failed to notice. He was a slim man in his early forties, with a sallow face, only slightly pockmarked. He had a good figure and a sparkling pair of liquid brown eyes in a thin and clever face.

Effy justified the luxury of French lessons by hiring him for only two hours a week, thus being able to persuade herself it was not a very great expense.

She had just finished one of her lessons when the squire was announced. Amy was out walking with Delilah. Effy soothed the squire's troubles by explaining that Delilah had initially been most upset to find they, the Tribbles, were not old friends at all, but merely earning their living, but that, once the initial row was over, Delilah appeared to have settled down.

The squire's face cleared. "Then I can count myself the happiest man in England. I owe a great debt of gratitude to Miss Amy. I am to be married."

"Congratulations," said Effy faintly. "Does my sister know of this?"

"I am looking forward to telling her," said Mr. Wraxall.

Effy felt quite sick. So Amy was to be married. What on earth would she do now? She would be very lonely without Amy.

"Are you sure you are making the right decision, Mr. Wraxall?" said Effy. "Surely no one can take the place of your beloved wife. And then, would it not be better to wait until Delilah has set up her own household?"

"Delilah will understand. I thought I should never feel at ease with a lady again," said the squire, "but Miss Amy changed all that."

Effy felt like crying. Amy would not care. Amy would be so happy and excited she would leave the house in Holles Street without a backward glance. It was terrible that Amy, plain Amy, should be the first of them to get married after all these years.

Delilah and Amy entered the room at that moment. Delilah flew into her father's arms. Amy and Effy tactfully withdrew to leave them alone.

As Effy had already explained, Delilah had lost all her initial fury at finding the Tribbles were being paid for their services, but she could not help asking plaintively, "Am I so very bad, Papa?"

"No, my chuck. But I am deeply concerned for you. I would like to see my grandchildren before I die. I cannot help feeling your continuing independence is in part my fault. I should have encouraged you more to find a suitable partner."

"It has been borne in on me I am judged to be a heartbreaker, Papa. My only quarrel with you is that you might have told me sooner what everyone was saying about me."

"What people say about you does not matter to me," said the squire, "and I confess, for a long time I put such gossip down to jealousy. But if you are content with your home life and if the idea of marriage is really repugnant to you, then you may return with me this day."

Delilah found to her surprise that she did not want to return . . . yet. She was enjoying her life in London. Besides, she had not seen Sir Charles since the day of the picnic, and it was important that she see him again to show him how indifferent she was to him.

"Perhaps another month," she said. "Who knows? I may find a beau yet."

"Have you anyone in mind?"

Delilah laughed. "I thought I had. There is a certain Lord Andrew Bergrave who was courting me, but it appears he is a hardened gambler and so I have been trying to keep out of his way. I suppose he *is* a hardened gambler, but I cannot help feeling that it was Sir Charles who went out of his way to make him appear so."

"Perhaps Sir Charles was concerned for your welfare."

"Not he."

"I think you do him an injustice. It is not that he is enamoured of you, rather that he feels a loyalty to someone from our village. I, too, would feel compelled to step in if I met a young lady from Hoppleton and thought she was about to plunge into a bad match."

"I detest Sir Charles. He has too high an opinion of his attractions."

"People might say the same about you."

"Why do you always defend him?"

"I think you are too hard on him. He is a level-headed and sensible young man."

"Hardly young!" exclaimed Delilah.

"You will soon be wearing caps yourself," pointed out the squire brutally.

"Pooh! There is no need to try to *frighten* me into marriage," said Delilah.

"Now, listen to me," said the squire. "I have great news. I am to be married!"

"Well, it is not so much of a surprise," said Delilah. She had grown to like Amy, but she had to admit she did not relish the idea of surrendering the reins of household government to anyone else.

"You knew of my affection?" cried the squire. "It is only I who was blind. It took Miss Amy to open my eyes."

"Does Miss Amy know?" asked Delilah. "Have you . . . ?"

"Not yet," said the squire.

"Then I shall fetch her."

Delilah soon returned with Amy. "But bring Miss Effy here as well," said the squire. "I want everyone to hear this."

Looking surprised, Delilah went to fetch Effy. Amy curtsied to the squire, blushed slightly and went and sat down, trying to look demure and modest.

Effy came in. She had a sudden premonition that Amy had made a terrible mistake and went to stand behind her sister and place a comforting hand on her shoulder.

"I have great pleasure in announcing my forthcoming marriage," said the squire. "It is thanks to you, Miss Amy, that I have found happiness."

Effy relaxed her grip on Amy's shoulder. But it was an odd sort of way of making a proposal.

"You may be assured, Mr. Wraxall, that the lady is delighted to accept you," said Amy.

"Well," laughed the squire, "that was indeed the case, but I did not expect to be so lucky. I had long enjoyed the company of Mrs. Cavendish without being aware of it. I was frightened and shy in the company of ladies. Then I met you, Miss Amy, so direct, so honest, such a good chap that somehow it put my fears to rest. Yes, I proposed to Mrs. Cavendish, a widow in our village, ladies, and she accepted."

Delilah looked at Amy's stricken face. She had been about to cry out "Mrs. Cavendish!" but that look on Amy's face stopped her. For Amy's sake, the news must be accepted without surprise.

Amy rose to her feet. Effy put an arm around her sister's waist. "I am pleased and I congratulate you," said Amy. "I wish you and Mrs. Cavendish well. Pray excuse us. We are sure you have much to discuss."

Effy and Amy walked from the room.

Delilah listened until she was sure they were well out of earshot and then she rounded on her father. "Men!" she cried. "Did you or did you not tell Miss Amy she had made you think of marriage?"

"Of course I did. Have I not explained? It was she who made me feel at ease with women again."

"And you call *me* a heart-breaker!" said Delilah bitterly. "You led that poor lady to believe you meant to propose marriage to her."

"I could not," said the squire. "Oh, if that is the case, I must apologize to her directly."

"No, you must not," said Delilah. "That would be even more humiliating. Did you not think she had feelings?"

"I thought of her as a good friend," said the squire mournfully.

"I will try to comfort her as best I can," said Delilah. "Now to talk of your marriage . . ."

The squire was only too eager to forget about Amy and talk about Mrs. Cavendish. Before he left, he said he would stay the night at Limmer's Hotel and return to the country in the morning.

After he had gone, Delilah sat deep in thought. She was very fond of Mrs. Cavendish and thought the marriage very suitable. On the other hand, Mrs. Cavendish was an excellent housekeeper. Delilah would be left idle. All her tasks—tending the vegetable garden, making jams and pickles and cordials, visiting the poor and sick—would all be taken over by Mrs. Cavendish. For the first time in her life, Delilah began to find the idea of an establishment of her own attractive.

She went upstairs to look for Amy and met Effy on the landing. "Silly woman," said Effy, meaning Amy. "She will not let me comfort her but sits there, drinking brandy, and saying she knew all along about this Mrs. Cavendish and had only said the squire was going to marry her to tease me."

Effy went on downstairs and Delilah ran up to Amy's room and went inside.

"Hey, ho!" said Amy, her eyes bright and feverish. "Have some brandy."

"Thank you," said Delilah. Amy handed her a glass. "To the happy pair," she said. Delilah drank the toast and then refilled her glass and raised it. She looked at Amy. "To me and you, Miss Amy," she said, "and all poor, broken-hearted rejected women everywhere."

Delilah suddenly put down her glass and her eyes filled with tears. It came back to her in a rush, all the feelings of humiliation and sadness that Sir Charles's rejection of her had caused. She had never cried over it, but now she did and felt she could not stop. Tears began to pour down Amy's leathery cheeks as well, and both women cried unchecked for a long time.

"That's better," said Amy at last. "Much better. Thank you for making me cry, Delilah."

"And thank you, too, Amy," said Delilah, dropping the title of "Miss," for she felt she and Amy were sisters in affliction.

Amy refilled the glasses. "A pox on all men," she said.

"Confusion to 'em," said Delilah, knocking back her drink in one gulp.

When Effy entered sometime later, it was to find both of them fast asleep in their chairs, with the empty brandy decanter between them. Clucking with dismay, Effy summoned the servants to help her get both somnolent drunks to bed.

Monsieur Duclos wondered whether to inform Miss Effy Tribble that she would never master his language. Effy had not been taught French in her youth, and it looked as if she would never be taught now. But most of the ladies he instructed murdered his language. All they really wanted were a few phrases with which to lard their conversation, as was the fashion. He liked the Tribbles and did not want to cheat them in any way, but they paid well and he needed the money. Also, there was one of his countrywomen in the house, Yvette, the dressmaker. She had entered the room once when Effy was having her lesson, carrying a roll of silk to ask Effy's opinion on the colour. Monsieur Duclos had addressed her in French, starting to ask her questions, but before she could reply, Effy had dismissed her with a wave of her hand.

The French teacher now often wondered where the seamstress had her room and whether she was ever allowed any time off. He took to haunting Holles Street in his free time, but never once did he see Yvette leave the house. He tried to befriend the servants in the hope of finding one willing to carry a message, but the servants distrusted him because he was French and shied away from him.

If he had been teaching Amy, Monsieur Duclos might have felt bold enough to broach the subject of Yvette. But it was Effy who was his pupil. Effy flirted with him, and Monsieur Duclos knew the value of keeping his middle-aged pupils happy. At least Effy was pretty and dainty and not like Mrs. Cullen, the wife of a colonel, also one of his pupils, who was fat and gross and breathed heavily and found every excuse she could to lean against him while pretending to study her books.

He was just leaving the drawing-room a week after the disastrous news of the squire's forthcoming marriage when he felt he was being watched and glanced up the stairs. There, at the turn of the stair, stood Yvette, looking down on him.

He glanced quickly about and then bounded up the stairs to Yvette. "Where can we talk?" he asked. "Follow me," she said softly, and led the way to her room.

Mr. Haddon returned to Holles Street and to a great welcome from Amy and Effy. He gratefully sank back into the comfort of all the old flattery and attention and then asked how Miss Wraxall was getting along.

"She is behaving very prettily," said Amy. "We have nothing to complain of. Quite a reformed character. We have, in fact, become very close friends."

But Delilah had a plot, a plot she had no intention of telling Amy about. She remembered her father's words, that Sir Charles, like himself, would be anxious if anyone from their village showed signs of being about to make a bad match. To that end, she had been talking at balls and parties to other débutantes, finding out, not who was suitable, but who was entirely unsuitable. At certain of these functions, she saw Sir Charles, but he did not come near her and that spurred Delilah on to action.

Delilah could have gained the information she needed much more quickly had she been a wallflower and had spent more time with the other débutantes. As it was, it took her a whole month to learn that the most dangerous man on the London scene was Mr. Guy Berkeley. On the

face of it, Mr. Berkeley was a catch. He did not look at all
sinister. He was in his late twenties, rich, handsome, and
had an open and engaging manner. He was tall, with hair
as black as Delilah's own; he had deep-blue eyes and a
good figure and a square face and strong chin. His nose
bordered on the snub, a small defect in an otherwise perfect appearance. He was a heart-breaker. He was a philanderer. Worse, he did not just flirt, he seduced. His
charm lay in the fact that for a brief spell he genuinely fell
in love with his victims. He had enough money for parents to persuade themselves that the rumours about him
were untrue, and enough looks and charm for their
daughters to wish to be just as blind. He was a close friend
of the Prince Regent, which was the reason he had been
forgiven all.

Sir Charles was not present at the ball where Delilah
first met Mr. Berkeley, but Lord Andrew was. He had
ruefully accepted that he had no hope with Delilah, but
he was startled to notice that Delilah, who had appeared
to have given up flirting, was behaving quite disgracefully
with Mr. Berkeley. Amy did not see it. Effy had the headache and had stayed at home, and Mr. Haddon, who had
been invited, had escorted Amy. They talked and talked
like the old friends they were and forgot about Delilah.
Amy was now so used to Delilah behaving herself that
she had ceased to watch her every move.

Lord Andrew broached the subject of Delilah with Sir
Charles the next day. "Miss Wraxall was flirting quite
shamelessly at the ball last night," he said crossly.

Sir Charles looked amused. "Miss Wraxall usually flirts
shamelessly," he said. "Who was her victim?"

"I think, in this case, she is the victim but does not
know it. Mr. Guy Berkeley."

"Who is he? Oh, I remember. One of Prinny's cronies."

"And that friendship is why he is still in this country instead of hiding away on the Continent from irate parents. He is a womanizer. His last victim was little Miss Pettifor. She tried to kill herself, but her parents stepped in, and gossip has it that Prinny stepped in, too, and a marriage with Lord Carey—you know him, always in need of money—was arranged. Miss Pettifor went to the altar heavily pregnant, and it is highly doubtful that the child was his, for he had not set eyes on the girl until a fortnight before the wedding, or so it was believed. Special licence. Rushed job of work."

"I have no doubt someone will soon put Miss Wraxall wise," said Sir Charles. "I cannot imagine those two dragons she lives with allowing her to make a cake of herself."

"Guy Berkeley is rich and good ton," said Lord Andrew. "You would be amazed how many people are prepared to believe only the best of him. The Town is thin of eligibles at the moment."

"I am persuaded that Miss Wraxall has a good amount of common sense," said Sir Charles.

"I overheard Berkeley offering to take her driving today," said Lord Andrew. "Why don't you go along to the Park this afternoon and have a look at 'em?"

"I think it's a case of if you can't have her, then you're not going to allow anyone else a chance," said Sir Charles.

"And I could have had her, my friend, had you not introduced me to a dice game."

"Come, now, confess your only interest in her was her money."

"No, I cannot confess that. You seem blissfully unaware that your village maiden has taken the Town by storm. She is the most beautiful creature anyone has seen this age."

Sir Charles felt annoyed. When he was not with Delilah, he remembered her only as the rather plump and endearing seventeen-year-old of so long ago. He had, he admitted, kept out of her road, but it had piqued him that she did not appear to have noticed that fact, or even to have been aware that he was in the room.

"I suppose," he said slowly, "it is my duty to make sure she does not make a fool of herself. Perhaps I shall go to the Park, although I doubt if I shall be able to find her in all the press."

But he had no difficulty at all in finding Delilah. Mr. Guy Berkeley was driving a showy swan-necked phaeton as high as the first storey of a house. Beside him sat Delilah, so entranced with Mr. Berkeley's company that she seemed unaware of the sensation she was causing or that several gentlemen were standing on their chairs to get a better look at her.

Sir Charles felt himself becoming furious. Delilah was behaving like a demi-rep. As a friend of her father's, the least he could do would be to call at Holles Street and read her a lecture.

Before he reached there, Amy and Effy were already discussing Mr. Berkeley. "I do not know what Delilah is doing encouraging that young man," said Effy. "I find he has a bad reputation. How could you bring yourself to give him permission to take Delilah driving?"

"I trust Delilah," said Amy. "She is merely enjoying herself. She has not taken a serious liking to any gentleman so far."

"But our job is to see that she does," said Effy crossly. "I should have gone to that ball, but my headache was quite terrible. Poor Mr. Haddon! How he must have missed me."

"I don't think he even noticed you weren't there," said Amy. "We had so much to talk about."

"He must have noticed and asked the reason for my absence," said Effy, "for I received such a pretty bouquet of flowers from him this morning."

Amy felt as if she had been plunged into cold water. Mr. Haddon had never sent *her* flowers.

"You must stop this ridiculous business of fancying men to be in love with you," said Amy. "Only look at the way you flirt with that French tutor. How can you expect Delilah to behave when you set such a bad example?"

"I do not flirt with Monsoor Duclos," said Effy. "He admires my mind."

"It is part of his business to flatter his silly clients," said Amy. "I don't know what you want to speak French for anyway."

"*C'est toot la maud,*" said Effy crossly.

"Whatever that means," said Amy. "I hear Delilah now."

Delilah came in. She was about to ask the sisters what Monsieur Duclos was doing descending from the upper regions at this time of day, but Amy made her forget the Frenchman.

"I have to tell you," said Amy roundly, "that Berkeley ain't suitable."

"Why?" asked Delilah, unpinning her bonnet.

"He seduces gels, he don't marry 'em."

"Perhaps he has never been in love," said Delilah.

"I suppose that's what he told you," said Amy cynically. "Be warned, Delilah. One minute he'll be paying you pretty compliments, and the next, he'll have his leg over you."

"Amy!" screamed Effy, fanning herself vigorously.

"Odd's cock-fools! I speak the truth," said Amy, losing her temper, not really over Delilah and Mr. Berkeley but because of those flowers Mr. Haddon had sent Effy.

"Sir Charles Digby," announced Harris.

Amy noticed the sudden look of satisfaction on Delilah's face.

Sir Charles came in, made his bow to the ladies, and then said, "I would like a few words in private with Miss Wraxall."

The sisters hesitated. "I am an old friend of the family," said Sir Charles. "Pray allow me only a little time."

The sisters exchanged glances and then Amy said, "Well, only a few minutes, mind. And leave the door open."

"What is it you wish to speak to me about?" asked Delilah as soon as they were alone.

"I am come to warn you about Mr. Berkeley," said Sir Charles.

"Pooh!" said Delilah. "You are come too late. I have just *been* warned."

Sir Charles's face cleared. "Of course I might have known I could rely on the Misses Tribble."

"I find Mr. Berkeley very engaging company," said Delilah airily, "and I never listen to rumour."

"Now, don't be silly . . ."

"How dare you address me in such a tone, sir! I am not a schoolgirl. Nay! Neither am I an innocent seventeen-year-old, prepared to listen any more to your long and boring monologues. So tiresome in the country, is it not? One has so little choice of gentlemen that one finds oneself putting up with the most awful bores."

"For the friendship and affection I have for your father, Miss Wraxall, I will not stand by and see you make a fool of yourself. I put it to you plain. Mr. Berkeley means to take your virginity, not your hand in marriage."

"Perhaps he cannot take what has already been lost," said Delilah lightly.

Sir Charles's face flamed and he seized her by the arms and glared down into her eyes. "Are you trying to tell me that . . . ?" he began threateningly.

Delilah laughed. "I am not trying to tell you anything, sir. I am simply trying to shock you into taking your boring and interfering presence elsewhere."

He looked down at her laughing, mocking eyes. He muttered something and crushed her in his arms and kissed her hard on the mouth, a punishing kiss that ended up punishing the punisher as Delilah's lips melted and burned against his own and her body became soft and pliant in his. He could have gone on kissing her until the end of time, but a screech of "Sir Charles!" from two outraged voices made him release her quickly and step back.

Amy and Effy stood at the entrance to the drawing-room, looking as if they could not believe their eyes.

"Is there not something you have failed to ask us, Sir Charles?" demanded Amy sternly.

Delilah had turned away and walked to the window. Sir Charles looked at her in a bemused way and then looked back to the sisters. His own voice seemed in his ears to be coming from very far away.

"I beg your pardon, ladies," he said. "Pray give me leave to pay my addresses to Miss Wraxall."

Amy and Effy beamed with pleasure. Delilah slowly turned around.

"No, Sir Charles," she said. "I don't want you."

Sir Charles made a stiff jerky bow and walked from the room.

"Oh, dear," said Amy weakly. "Let me sit down."

"Will you never stop flirting?" raged Effy. "You had no right to let that poor man kiss you and then turn you down flat."

"*He* kissed *me*," said Delilah. "I didn't kiss him."

"Well, now you've got your revenge," said Amy, "we can all be happy."

Delilah burst into tears and ran from the room.

"Some folks never really know what they want or who they want," muttered Amy, and went after Delilah to see what on earth was the matter with her.

Chapter 6

. . . there is nothing better than skating. I
should be very glad to cut eights and nines with
his lordship, but the only figure I should cut
would be that of as many feet as would measure
my own length on the ice.

Thomas Love Peacock

AS IF TO COMPENSATE for a lazy, sunny autumn, grim, freezing winter descended on London, bringing with it choking seas of fog or hard white frosts that turned the buildings into black-and-white etchings. The skeletal trees in the parks looked so stiff and frozen, you would think a puff of wind would make them shiver into so many brittle pieces of kindling. Smoke belched up from thousands of chimneys, which caused a gentle rain of soot to fall on nobleman and pauper alike.

Conversation during calls was usually about the best way to clean clothes. Sometimes the fog was so thick, it crept into the houses and lay in smoky layers on the chilly air. Winter brought back the great fear of consumption as tubercular coughs racked the city.

And yet, to Delilah, who felt she had become truly Londonized, there was something exciting about the fog, about venturing out at night into that great floating grey sea to end up in some glittering ballroom or salon where the rich had tried to recreate summer with great roaring fires and banks of hothouse flowers.

She kept Mr. Guy Berkeley dancing attendance on her. Amy and Effy did not put a brake on Delilah's goings-on, as they quickly discovered that, when Delilah was at her most flirtatious with Mr. Berkeley, Sir Charles Digby forgot to dance with anyone, but stood in some ballroom, staring at Delilah.

Amy had decided that Delilah was in love with Sir Charles. To her way of thinking, it was a perfectly sensible marriage prospect. Underneath it all, she still felt bruised by the squire's engagement to that Mrs. Cavendish. Sometimes Amy dreamt that the squire would be so pleased with her if she were to be instrumental in bringing Sir Charles and Delilah together that he would forget about the Widow Cavendish and realize it was she, Amy, he had wanted all along. Her hurt and her dreams stopped her from competing with Effy for Mr. Haddon's favour, although she enjoyed that gentleman's company as much as ever. Mr. Haddon sensed this certain withdrawal of interest and did not like it. He was aware of things he would not have noticed before, things like a certain anger in Amy because he had sent Effy flowers. He had tried to compensate by sending Amy a gift of a new book, just out, on the habits and customs of the American Indian. He had been there when Amy had unwrapped her present. He was sure she was disappointed. It was a fine book. What had she expected?

The truth was Amy *had* been disappointed. Flowers were romantic, books were not. She had been hoping for a piece of jewellery or something romantic to put Effy in her place. It was that dull present of the book which had set Amy dreaming about the squire again, and so that simple and straightforward country gentleman became imbued in Amy's mind with all sorts of romantic passions he not only did not have, but had never had. If Mrs. Cavendish had caused the squire to tremble and feel exhilarated in her company, then he would never have proposed to her. Marriage to the squire simply meant companionship.

Amy had decided she must do something to bring matters between Sir Charles and Delilah a little further forward. Skating was all the rage and the Serpentine was frozen solid. Amy knew that Delilah could skate, and hoped that Sir Charles could also skate and that Mr. Guy Berkeley could not. She proposed to Effy that they arrange a skating party.

Effy was at first horrified. She herself could not skate and the idea of sitting at the edge of the Serpentine in the middle of a black winter's evening seemed the height of folly, but Mr. Haddon was enthusiastic, so Effy gave in with good grace and ordered Yvette to trim a red woollen gown with the fur from an old pelisse. Yvette saved the sisters a considerable amount of money by occasionally altering their old gowns and making them look like completely new and different ones.

Delilah was praying there would be no fog. Fog would mean the party would have to be cancelled. Amy had not told Delilah that Sir Charles had been invited. Delilah did not expect to see him, therefore, and was looking forward to an evening without being haunted by him. He had started to invade her dreams, and in the latest one he had come to her naked and had made violent and passionate love to her. The dream had been so vivid that Delilah—although her want of experience had kept the fantasy embraces passionate but innocent—felt sure she could never look at Sir Charles Digby again without blushing.

She was amused by Mr. Berkeley's company and considered him to be no risk whatever. Mr. Berkeley's reputation was such that no one ever credited him with having any more feeling towards his victims than a master of foxhounds has towards the fox. But Mr. Berkeley was very much attracted by Delilah, an attraction that was on the verge of becoming an obsession.

Like all true philanderers, he usually fell in love with his victims. That was what made him so attractive, so dangerous. But never before had he been so violently attracted to any woman as he was to Delilah.

Unlike Delilah, he prayed for fog, a fog that would descend when the party was in progress. He might be able to skate off somewhere with Delilah and steal a kiss.

But the evening of the party was clear and frosty with a thin winter's disc of a moon sailing above the Serpentine. Braziers of coals were burning beside the lake, and Effy, in her new fur-trimmed gown and wrapped in an enormous fur cloak, sat shivering by one and hoping the party would not last very long. She was at a disadvantage. Amy could skate and she could not. It transpired Mr. Haddon could skate. The servants from Holles Street, under the direction of Harris, the butler, had set up a long table at the edge of the ice to serve the guests with hot punch and delicacies. Skating was a democratic sport and the servants were to be allowed to join in the fun once their duties of supplying the guests with food and drink were over; it was quite usual at skating parties for the uppers to lend the lowers their skates.

"I don't like to think of Yvette being alone in the house," said Amy to Effy, as she bent forward to tie on her skates. "She has become quiet and pale of late. Do you know, I was just thinking the other day that she has hardly had any time off, nor asked for it. I think she is in need of a holiday. Perhaps if Delilah does not marry and returns to the country, we could lend Yvette to her for a little. Yvette says she is very well, but it is very hard to know what she is thinking."

"I really don't believe she thinks of very much," said Effy. "She is quite content, and I left her plenty of sewing to keep her busy. Such a prim little thing. She is happier when occupied."

At that moment, Yvette was lying naked in the arms of Monsieur Duclos. Before she succumbed to another wave of passion, she thought of all the sewing Effy had left her. It would mean sitting up during the night trying to get it finished after Monsieur Duclos had left.

Mr. Guy Berkeley arrived late. He had been drinking with friends during the afternoon in a tavern in Holborn in an upstairs room. On leaving, he had fallen down the stairs and sprained his ankle. His servants carried him in a chair to the edge of the ice. Delilah exclaimed in dismay but showed no signs of abandoning skating to stay beside him.

And then Sir Charles Digby skated up to where Delilah was standing beside Mr. Berkeley, bowed and said, "Would you care to take a turn on the ice with me, Miss Wraxall?"

All in that moment, Delilah forgot how much she hated him. The air was crisp and full of the heady smells of punch and charcoal, sweetmeats and pineapple. Little lanterns had been hung among the trees.

Arm in arm, Sir Charles and Delilah glided off. She

could feel the strength of his arm and was aware of the coloured lanterns and faces of the guests flying past, of the hiss of skates over the ice, of the splendid surprise of seeing Mr. Haddon of all people cut a neat figure eight, and felt a tremendous rush of happiness.

When they slowed their pace, Delilah said impulsively, "I am so sorry I was rude to you. But you should not have kissed me."

He glided to a stop and then swung to face her. "I did propose marriage, Miss Wraxall. My intentions were honourable. But your apology is accepted. I in turn apologize for having kissed you. There. Now we can be comfortable again."

Mr. Berkeley anxiously watched the pair from his seat at the edge of the lake. Delilah would soon return. She would not want to occasion talk by skating with the one man all evening. But, to his irritation, the pair moved off again, slowly this time, deep in conversation.

He kept his eyes fastened on them. What were they saying? She must return soon. She could not continue to ignore him. And, oh heavens, it seemed as if his prayers were to be answered. A mist was beginning to veil the scene and that mist had that particularly acrid smell which told Mr. Berkeley that there was every possibility it would soon thicken into fog.

"Do you miss Hoppleton?" Sir Charles was asking.

"Yes," said Delilah. "I miss things as they were. But I am soon to have a stepmother."

"Indeed! Who is Mr. Wraxall to marry?"

"Mrs. Cavendish."

"Well, that is splendid. A perfect match. You will have a stepmother who is already a friend."

"Unfortunately, Mrs. Cavendish is a good housekeeper and most of my duties will fall to her," said Delilah. "Hey, ho! The only solution is to set up my own establishment."

"With Mr. Berkeley?"

"Perhaps," said Delilah. "Why not?"

"He is not the man for you, nor the man for any respectable female."

"Mr. Berkeley is all that is pleasant. I swear I am half in love with him already," said Delilah.

Sir Charles was furious. He wanted to shake her. They skated on in silence, Delilah not noticing that the fog was thickening rapidly or that he was guiding her away from the lights of the party. One of her skates struck a twig embedded in the ice and she stumbled. His arm slid about her waist.

"There is no need to hold me so tightly, Sir Charles," said Delilah. Delilah remembered that dream and her face grew hot.

She then realized the sounds of the party were faint and that they had moved off into the darkness, a darkness quite thick as the fog came down around them.

She stopped. "Take me back, Sir Charles," she said in a small voice, suddenly afraid of him and the effect he had on her body.

. He had stopped at the same time but kept one arm tightly about her waist. "I shall let you go," he said, "when you have promised me to have nothing further to do with Guy Berkeley."

"I do not belong to you," retorted Delilah, trying to pull away. "I shall marry Mr. Berkeley if it pleases me."

"I think you do belong to me," he said slowly. "I think we belong to each other and I think I have been a very great fool not to realize it before."

"I am cold," whispered Delilah. "The Tribbles will be looking for me."

"Marry me!"

"No," said Delilah bleakly, remembering all her previous hurt. "You are cold and haughty and unfeeling—"

"Unfeeling!" he cried. "Lady, I am all feeling."

He caught her chin in one hand and, still holding her clipped round the waist, he kissed her fiercely. Her lips were cold and stiff. He continued to kiss her, stifling her protests with his mouth, until her lips grew soft and responsive beneath his own. The emotions that engulfed Delilah were so fierce that tears began to run down her face. "Don't cry," he whispered, kissing her tears. "Please don't cry. Kiss me again. You bewitch me, Delilah."

He took out his handkerchief and gently dried her cheeks. She smiled up at him tremulously.

"I cannot see your face," she said shakily. "The fog is so thick."

"Then feel my lips again," he said huskily. With an odd little sound, she turned her face up to his and her lips melted into his own.

Mr. Guy Berkeley had hobbled all over the ice in search of them, cursing the fog he had prayed so earnestly for earlier that evening. He almost bumped into them. They were wrapped so tightly together that he was about to mutter an apology and limp past. Some vulgar courting couple, he thought. And then he heard Delilah's voice, a broken little voice, saying pleadingly, "I think we had better go back. Please release me. I cannot think when you hold me so tightly."

"Do as she says!" grated Mr. Berkeley.

The couple broke apart.

"I wish you bumpkins would stay in the country," said Mr. Berkeley to Sir Charles. "Let her go, you lout. Let her go."

"Miss Wraxall is free," said Sir Charles haughtily. "Take yourself off, Berkeley. You are decidedly *de trop.*"

112

Mr. Berkeley drew off his gloves and struck Sir Charles across the face with them. "Cur!" he snarled.

"I demand satisfaction," said Sir Charles.

"Gladly. Come, Miss Wraxall," said Mr. Berkeley.

Delilah shrank away from him. "What are you doing?" she cried.

Sir Charles said, "We are about to arrange a duel. Do not sound so distressed, my sweet. Every beautiful lady should have a duel fought over her."

"Delilah!" came Amy's voice.

"Over here!" called Sir Charles and Amy came skating up.

"Take Miss Wraxall away," said Sir Charles. "Mr. Berkeley and I have much to discuss."

"Stop them," cried Delilah. "They are going to fight a duel."

"I trust you will remember Miss Wraxall's reputation," said Amy sternly.

"I am sure we will both do that," replied Sir Charles. "Please leave us."

Amy pulled the reluctant Delilah away.

Sir Charles and Mr. Berkeley proceeded to discuss seconds, time, place, and weapons.

"What can I do?" asked Delilah, as Amy led her through the choking fog back to the party.

"You can help me to get Effy home, for a start," said Amy. "What were you thinking of to skate off into the fog and disappear like that? I thought you didn't like Sir Charles."

"But the duel! We must stop the duel."

"Can't be done," said Amy. "Gentlemen are funny about their duels. It would be like trying to break into White's and stop a card game. Not done. Impossible. I myself did once . . ." Amy broke off, remembering the

113

time that Mr. Haddon had fought a duel over Effy and she herself had dressed up as a Bow Street Runner and had tried to stop it.

"Come home," urged Amy instead. "There is nothing we can do now."

The duel had been fixed in two days' time at eight-thirty in the morning on Parliament Hill Fields. The weapons were pistols. In the white-hot heat of jealousy, Mr. Berkeley felt sure he could trounce this nobody from the country. But to be sure, and when the first fire had died down, he asked about the clubs the next day for information on Sir Charles Digby. With a sinking heart, he heard that Sir Charles was accounted one of the bravest soldiers in Wellington's army. Mr. Berkeley decided he had better not go ahead with the duel. He would ask the Prince Regent to use his power in some way to advise Sir Charles to leave Town. But the Prince Regent, increasingly fat and increasingly fickle, had become irritated with Mr. Berkeley. That gentleman had failed to dance attendance on him of late, had failed to remember to send the usual flattering gifts. An audience was denied.

Mr. Berkeley thought gloomily of the character of his seconds. He had asked a Mr. Withering and a certain Lord Pomfrey to second him and they had agreed. He knew it was no use trying to get them to persuade Sir Charles to drop the duel. Both were looking forward to it immensely. He was furious with that minx, Delilah. She had no right to play such tricks on him. Mr. Berkeley was determined to stay alive, if only to get his revenge on her. In his fear, he decided she had deliberately led him on, only to embroil him in a silly fight for his life. He almost forgot he was the instigator of the duel.

The evening before the duel, he was desperate. He took himself off to one of Covent Garden's most disreputable taverns. He was not unknown there and was acquainted with several of the villains who frequented the place. He found the sort of unsavoury character he needed and bribed the man heavily. His new helper was to conceal himself on Parliament Hill Fields and as soon as Sir Charles raised his pistol, this man was to shoot him dead before Sir Charles could pull the trigger. It would be assumed the bullet came from Mr. Berkeley's pistol.

Feeling much more cheerful, Mr. Berkeley went back to his lodgings to get a good night's sleep.

Delilah felt she could not bear to sit quietly at home waiting for news. She did not know where the duel was to be held. She knew the time would probably be around dawn. But even if she knew the duelling place, she could not hope to get there, for she had no means of transport. In vain did she beg the sisters to alert the authorities. Amy shook her head and said if she did that, Sir Charles would get to hear who had told on him, and would never speak to Delilah again.

It was a freezing night, although there was no fog. Amy and Effy went early to bed. Delilah paced up and down her room, feeling utterly helpless. She was afraid for Sir Charles and afraid of him at the same time. He had such power over her. It would be terrifying to be married to him, to be such a slave to any man. Before, when she was seventeen, Delilah had often dreamt of marriage to Sir Charles, but she had imagined a tranquil existence enlivened with a few sweet kisses, never that her body would so fiercely yearn for his that she felt half mad.

She fell asleep at last in a chair and awoke at six in the morning, hearing the dreary, hoarse voice of the watch calling the hour. Delilah made up her mind. She simply had to take some sort of action. She dressed in a plain warm gown and wrapped herself in her thickest, drabbest cloak and wound a scarf about her hair. The squire kept his daughter generously supplied with pin-money. Delilah put a rouleau of guineas in her pocket and then made her way slowly down the stairs and quietly unlocked the front door and slipped out into the street.

She walked down to Oxford Street and waited patiently, hoping not to be surprised by a party of bloods, until she heard the clip-clop of horse's hooves and saw a hack approaching.

The Jehu listened in surprise as she said she wished him to wait at the corner of Brook Street until he saw a carriage leaving and to follow it. He started to shake his head but she produced the rouleau of guineas, extracted two and held them up so that they glittered faintly in the moonlight.

" 'Op in," growled the driver.

Delilah heaved a sigh of relief. The first part was over.

They waited at the corner of Brook Street, Delilah standing beside the carriage. The parish lamps were extinguished at twelve, but there was a full moon riding above. She did not know which was Lord Andrew's house but was sure anyone leaving so early in the morning must be Sir Charles. She shrank back into the shadow of the hack as a carriage drove into Brook Street and stopped outside one of the houses. A man got out, knocked at the door and was admitted. Delilah waited, shivering.

A carriage was brought around to the front door of the house by grooms from the mews. Then the house door opened again and Sir Charles came out, followed by Lord Andrew and the man Delilah had already seen.

"Won't do, miss," called down the driver. "If them's the carriages I'm suppose' to follow, I'll never keep up with 'em. Besides, even if I could, they'd see me following and I'm having no truck with the quality. Beat my head in they would fer the fun o' it."

"You *must* wait," hissed Delilah, but he whipped up his horse and cursed and drove off.

Without thinking, Delilah ran lightly towards the two waiting carriages. She reached Sir Charles's carriage just as it was moving off and tumbled headlong into the rumble at the back. The man who had first arrived on the scene was driving the carriage in front.

Delilah clung on desperately inside the rumble. The carriage was bowling along at a great rate. The only good thing about all the jolting and shaking was that it had stopped her shivering.

But just when she thought she was going to be sick, that she could not possibly endure another moment, the pace slowed.

She waited until the carriage stopped. It dipped and swayed as Sir Charles and Lord Andrew climbed down. She could hear the murmur of their voices, then the sound of another carriage, then Lord Andrew's voice saying clearly, "Here comes the surgeon."

Then the voices grew fainter as they moved away.

Delilah climbed out and stood behind the carriage, shivering.

The grass and trees were thick with hoar-frost, and a red sun low on the horizon turned everything fiery-red.

Delilah peered around the carriage. Sir Charles, Lord Andrew and the other man, who must be Sir Charles's other second, were standing waiting. She looked about. There was a copse of trees quite near where they were standing. She began to creep towards it, finally coming to rest against the thick trunk of an oak.

All at once she felt completely and utterly helpless. She

had left Holles Street on impulse. Perhaps at the back of her mind had been some vague plan to throw herself between them. Now that she was here on the duelling ground, she knew that if she did such a thing, Sir Charles would never forgive her.

Mr. Berkeley arrived on the scene, accompanied by his seconds. A box of duelling pistols was produced. Both men took one each and weighed them in their hands and then gave them to their respective seconds for inspection. The surgeon squatted down on the grass and opened his case. He took out a sinister-looking scalpel that winked wickedly in the red sunlight and tested the edge with his thumb before returning it to the case.

The hammering of Delilah's heart slowed. A voice in her brain said over and over again, "There is nothing you can do."

The men stood back to back and then began to pace across the turf.

Sir Charles was hatless, his fair hair impeccably dressed, his cravat beautifully arranged. Mr. Berkeley was wearing a black coat buttoned up to the throat.

And then, just as they were turning to face each other, Delilah heard a sound from the other side of the tree. She crept around the thick bole.

There was a villainous-looking man standing there with a long pistol pointed straight at Sir Charles.

Delilah flung herself on him and screamed, "Murder!" at the top of her lungs. The man struck her to the ground and made his escape as everyone came running up.

Delilah jumped to her feet and pointed to the fleeing man. "He was trying to kill you, Charles," she gasped. "He was hiding here. He had a gun."

Lord Andrew flew off after the disappearing man, followed by Sir Charles. Delilah leaned against the trunk of the tree and closed her eyes and prayed she would not faint.

"My dear Miss Wraxall," came Mr. Berkeley's voice. "You should not have come here. That mad ruffian might have killed you."

Delilah opened her eyes and looked at him. "Are you sure you did not hire him to kill Sir Charles?"

"On my oath," cried Mr. Berkeley, "I would not dream of such a thing. I forgive the insult, Miss Wraxall, for you are evidently overwrought. Come, let . . ."

His voice trailed away and his face turned white, for coming towards them were Lord Andrew and Sir Charles, dragging the villain between them.

"Don't hurt me," screeched the man. "It was 'im, Berkeley, what paid me to do it."

Sir Charles released the man and walked straight up to Mr. Berkeley, drew back his fist and struck him full in the mouth.

Mr. Berkeley drew back and raised his duelling pistol. Delilah seized his arm and tried to bear it down. The gun went off with a loud report. Sir Charles caught Delilah and pulled her away. "Are you shot?" he asked.

"No," said Delilah shakily. "The bullet went into the ground."

"Stay there, and close your eyes," said Sir Charles quietly.

Delilah sank down weakly onto the ground. There came the sounds of blows and curses and then a long silence.

"Come, Delilah," came Sir Charles's voice.

She looked up. He was smiling down at her, his hand outstretched. He drew her to her feet.

She looked across the duelling ground. Mr. Guy Berkeley was lying full-length on the ground, blood running from his nose and mouth. "The surgeon will see to him," said Sir Charles. He turned to the seconds. "If Mr. Berkeley still wants satisfaction, you know where to find me. If you will excuse me, I will take Miss Wraxall home."

He helped her into his carriage, and then turned to her. "How did you get here?" he asked.

"In the rumble of your carriage," said Delilah, shivering, "and a very nasty experience it was too. I jumped in the back just as you were moving off."

He wrapped rugs about her. "I am sorry this is an open carriage. How did you know when I planned to leave?"

"I know duels are usually held at dawn," said Delilah, snuggling gratefully into the rugs. "I knew the sun would not rise until eight-thirty. I waited and waited outside your house with a hack. The driver promised me he would follow you, but when he saw your carriages, he said he could not possibly keep up, and even if he could, you would probably beat him. He seemed to have a sad opinion of the quality."

"Brave Delilah! Can it be you care for me a little?"

She had a bearskin rug drawn up over her nose and her large eyes looked up at him over the fur. "I would have done the same for anyone," she said, feeling miserably shy. His black eyes held a sensuous caressing look and her body was misbehaving again.

"Liar," he teased.

"C-can w-we go?" asked Delilah plaintively. "It is c-cold."

"Yes, my darling. Oh, Delilah!"

He tugged down the fur barrier from her mouth and fell to kissing her. She felt a sensation of drugged, heavy sweetness. His searching mouth roused more passion from her than she could have believed possible and his searching hands beneath the rugs sent liquid fire running through her body. Then he tore off his cravat and wrenched open his shirt and took her hand and placed it on his naked chest and whispered, "Do you hear how my heart beats for you?"

"It should not be like this," said Delilah. "You frighten me."

"This is what it is like when it is real," he said huskily, his lips against her hair.

"It cannot be," said Delilah. "I cannot marry you. I could not call my soul my own!"

"You *will* marry me. If I thought for a moment you would ever kiss any other man in the way you kiss me, then I would kill you. The fire will burn like this until I get you in my bed and in my arms, Delilah." He laughed. "Frustration is the only thing I find frightening."

Delilah struggled to explain. She felt she had lost her power over men. She had always called the tune. What if he left her again?

"I have been mistress of myself and my father's household since you left," she said. "You did not care a rap for me then. Why should you now?"

"I am not in the habit of begging ladies I don't give a rap for to marry me. But you need warmth and rest."

He buttoned his shirt and kissed her on the nose and then flapped the reins and the carriage began to bowl across the frosty turf.

When they reached Holles Street, he said, "I had better come in and give the Tribbles my apologies. They must have discovered your absence by now and be worried to death."

He called to a passing youth to guard his horses and threw him a guinea.

The door was opened by a little chambermaid who looked excited and flustered. "They've all gone out in the streets to look for you, miss," she gasped. "Miss Amy and Miss Effy and Mr. Harris have taken a carriage out to Chalk Farm and the rest's running around the streets. Even Miss Yvette's gone out."

"I will take Miss Wraxall up to her room," said Sir Charles. "She has had a bad shock."

"Why Chalk Farm?" asked Delilah as he led her up the stairs.

"That, my love, is where duels are normally held."

Delilah led the way into her room and then looked up at him shyly. "Thank you, Charles," she said.

"I shall stay until you are in bed," he replied. "Don't fuss. We are soon to be married, so what does it matter? Go behind that screen and undress."

Delilah felt too tired to argue. She undressed and put on a night-gown and wrapper and came round the screen and climbed into bed. He sat on a chair beside the bed, holding her hand until she fell asleep. He was tired himself and very grateful to be alive. His knuckles were grazed. He tucked the hand he had been holding under the bedclothes and went over to the toilet table and sponged his knuckles. He stretched and yawned and turned and looked at Delilah. How wonderful it would be to stretch out beside her and sleep.

Then he grinned. Why not? An hour's sleep and then he would go out and get a special licence. He walked round the bed and stretched out on top of the blankets. He felt under the bedclothes for Delilah and gathered her into his arms. She murmured sleepily but did not wake.

Amy and Effy erupting into the room half an hour later stopped short at the dreadful sight, and then came in and slammed the door on the faces of the gaping servants. Sir Charles came awake and sat up. Delilah slept on.

He put a finger to his lips and got out of bed and walked

quietly to the door of the room. The sisters followed him out.

"Not yet," he said in a whisper, "if you are going to shout at me, Miss Amy. I do not want Delilah to wake."

"My room!" said Amy curtly, pushing open a door opposite.

"Now!" she said, when she and Effy and Sir Charles were inside.

"Miss Wraxall is to marry me," said Sir Charles.

"I should hope so too," said Effy, her cheeks pink. "How could you . . . ?"

"I was lying on top of the bed with all my clothes on," said Sir Charles. "Miss Wraxall is still a virgin. She followed me out to the duelling ground at Parliament Hill Fields and there she saved my life. Berkeley had hired a ruffian to shoot me from behind a tree."

The sisters exclaimed and demanded to hear more. When he had finished, Amy said, "But there is to be no marriage by special licence, Sir Charles. We owe it to our reputation to do things in the proper manner. That means announcements in the newspapers and a proper wedding with all society there at St. George's, Hanover Square."

In vain did Sir Charles protest. Effy told him that if he was a proper gentleman, then he would be prepared to wait.

Sir Charles assured them at last that he would try to be patient and went off to purchase a special licence anyway.

The French tutor, Monsieur Duclos, was on his way later that day to Holles Street to give Miss Effy her lesson. The air was fresh and keen and he whistled as he walked along. He lived in modest lodgings in Bayswater and enjoyed the walk into Town. He was just approaching Tyburn Pike when to his surprise he heard himself being hailed.

A heavy travelling carriage lumbered to a stop on the other side of the road and there, leaning out of the window, was the Comte De Ville, a wealthy Frenchman who lived in Manchester Square. The colonel's wife to whom Monsieur Duclos gave French lessons lived next door to the comte. The Comte De Ville had always had a kind word for this lowly countryman of his when he met him coming and going to the colonel's. He knew, therefore, that Duclos was the son of a valet who had escaped the Terror with his family to seek refuge in England and that Duclos' parents were now dead and of how the French tutor dreamt of being able to return one day to his native country.

"Where are you bound, Monsieur Le Comte?" asked Duclos, looking at the great travelling carriage.

"Why, to France! I have hopes now of having my estates returned to me."

"I envy you from the bottom of my heart," said Duclos. "Oh, not for your estates, milor', but for the fact that you will soon be in that land which I think I will never see again."

"Then come with me," cried the comte. "I have need of a valet, my English fellow having refused to go. Come with me. I shall supply you with all the necessaries."

Duclos only hesitated for a moment. "Gladly," he said. The carriage door was opened and the tutor climbed in.

"Is there anyone you wish to write a note to?" asked the comte. "I have my travelling writing-case here."

"Yes, there is someone," said Duclos. The comte produced the writing-case and Duclos scribbled a hasty note to Yvette. "If this could be delivered," he said, "then I can leave with a free heart."

The comte glanced at the address and then, leaning out of the carriage window, called on a young man who was strolling past and gave him the letter and money to deliver it to Holles Street.

"That is that," said the comte. *"France, mon brave. En avant!"*

Amy rang the bell for the third time and for the third time asked Harris to go and fetch Yvette.

Harris came back with the same news. The dressmaker's door was locked. She did not reply. She must be asleep.

"Nonsense!" said Amy. "At this hour?"

She marched up the stairs and knocked on the door of Yvette's room.

Silence.

Amy rattled the handle and called out, but there was no reply.

Afterwards, Amy never knew why she did it, but there was suddenly something about that silence which unnerved her. She looked wildly about her until she saw a marble bust standing in a plinth in an alcove. She picked it up and swung it with all her force at the lock. There was a splintering of wood and the door swung open.

The French dressmaker was standing on a chair, a torn strip of sheet round her neck. A crumpled letter lay on the floor at her feet.

Amy went very carefully forward.

Yvette kicked away the chair, and, with a scream, Amy seized the swinging body and then howled for help at the top of her voice.

Chapter 7

Shut, shut the door, good John! fatigued, I said,
Tie up the knocker, say I'm sick, I'm dead, The
dog star rages! nay 'tis past a doubt, All
Bedlam, or Parnassus, is let out:

Alexander Pope

DELILAH WAS NEVER TO forget the extraordinary scene which followed the dressmaker's attempted suicide.

Yvette was lying on the sofa in the drawing-room, where she had been carried by the servants. Effy was weeping copiously and was having burnt feathers held under her nose by Baxter. The smell of burnt feathers was so pungent that Effy had to stop crying to exclaim, "I am *crying*, Baxter, not fainting." Amy was sitting, grimly reading the letter from Monsieur Duclos she had found on the floor of Yvette's room. And in the middle of all this, Mr. Haddon and Sir Charles were both announced.

Sir Charles had returned to tell the sisters and Delilah

that he was travelling immediately to Hoppleton to gain the squire's permission to marry Delilah as soon as possible in the local church. He had obtained a special licence. He understood the sisters' concern, their desire to have a fashionable wedding, but his wishes must come first.

The Tribbles barely heard him. Delilah was sitting in a chair by the sofa, holding the dressmaker's hand.

"Mr. Haddon," exclaimed Effy. "Such a to-do! Poor Yvette has tried to kill herself."

"Why?" asked Mr. Haddon.

"That French tutor of Effy's," said Amy bitterly. "He's been making love to her behind our backs and now he's gone off to France and left her."

"*Je suis enceinte,*" murmured Yvette weakly. "*Je suis sûr.*"

"What did she say?" demanded Amy.

Effy cleared her throat and said importantly, "She says she is sure she has scent on."

"I am afraid," said Sir Charles, "that what she actually said was that she is sure she is pregnant."

"Odd's fish!" said Amy, fanning herself with the letter. "How can you be sure? I mean, it's early days yet."

"Me, I know . . . here," said Yvette, pointing to her belly.

Delilah turned her beautiful eyes up to Sir Charles. "Perhaps Yvette could come with us to Hoppleton until the child is born—that is, if there is to be a child."

"As you wish," said Sir Charles, sounding far from enthusiastic.

"She should have considered what she was doing," said Mr. Haddon. He sounded much shocked. "I think, by her actions, she has taken herself out of your care, ladies."

Three pairs of eyes as hard as stones looked at the nabob. Instinctively the sisters and Delilah banded together against that cruel and unfeeling world of men, men who could not even begin to imagine the extent of Yvette's disgrace and shame.

A silence fell on the room. Effy's hand smoothed the silk of her gown, a gown made by Yvette, a gown which had been much envied by her contemporaries. What would they do without Yvette, whose clever needle created such fashions?

Delilah was thinking nervously of the cruelty of the world in general and the cruelty of men in particular. Sir Charles once more looked haughty and remote. She did not really know him, she thought. Perhaps after marriage he would turn out to be a tyrant.

Amy was thinking of the baby. It might be a little boy. It would be fun to have a child about the house. All through the years, Amy had longed for marriage and children. Now she was too old to have any children and it certainly seemed as if she would never marry.

"Adopt it," she said. She waved her arm in her excitement and sent a coffee-cup flying. "Yes, we'll adopt it, Effy."

"You could not," said Sir Charles. "You would need to be married."

"Then we'll just keep it here and look after it," said Amy impatiently. "What would you have us do? Turn Yvette off?"

"Let me kill myself," said Yvette weakly.

"You selfish girl," snapped Amy. "You will stay with us and have your baby, if there is a baby, and we will all bring it up together."

"We are too old to take on such a responsibility." Effy spoke quietly.

For one moment, Amy felt engulfed in despair. How fast the years were passing! As you got older, the faster the days and months began to race by. Then she thought again of the baby. How could anyone feel old with a baby in the house?

"It is *our* baby," she said fiercely. "Men are wicked and heedless. Come, Yvette, it is not the end of the world. You will have a strong, sturdy English boy."

"It might be a girl," pointed out Delilah, beginning to feel amused despite her concern for Yvette.

"A girl!" Effy sat up straight. "A girl," she said again. She could see in her mind's eye a pretty little creature like a doll, a doll to fuss over and dress in pretty clothes.

"I think Amy has the right of it," said Effy. "This does not call for dramatics, Yvette. Now, you must go to your room and rest. Life will go on as usual. You have been betrayed. But that's the French for you," added Effy, forgetting in the heat of the moment that the dressmaker was French herself. "No morals to speak of."

"I am glad that is settled," said Sir Charles. "May I have a few moments alone with my fiancée?"

"No, you may not," said Amy roundly. "There has been enough whoopsadaisy in this house already. You may speak to Delilah, but we will be present as well."

Sir Charles drew Delilah over to the window and said in a low voice, "I shall only be gone for a little. Please be careful. Berkeley is a foul creature and may want his revenge."

Delilah smiled. "As you can see, sir, I am well guarded."

"As to that, I am beginning to wonder whether the Tribbles are suitable chaperones for you. Ladies who cheerfully arrange to take care of a servant's bastard child are perhaps not the best people to instill good behaviour into débutantes."

"They are magnificent!" said Delilah fiercely. "Unless you can bring yourself to see the nobility of their actions, then I fear I cannot marry you!"

"My love . . ."

"And next time you come across a weeping, pregnant servant girl who is being turned into the streets without a character, think only that it is a mere accident of birth which prevents me from a similar fate."

"A lady would not dream . . ." he began. Then he flushed slightly under Delilah's steady gaze. "Never mind. I love you and we will be married." He kissed her on the cheek and left.

Baxter took Yvette back to her room, gave her a draft of laudanum, and then sat by the dressmaker's bed until she fell asleep.

Amy and Effy and Mr. Haddon talked in low voices. Delilah stood by the window of the drawing-room and watched Sir Charles walk off down the street below.

She was sorely troubled. Was this what marriage was going to be like? Would she not be allowed any thoughts of her own? Would she not be allowed to make any decisions? Passion was a cheat and a deceiver, and only look how it trapped poor women. She could not find it in her heart to blame Yvette.

Three days later, Lord Andrew was strolling down Bond Street when he saw Mr. Berkeley approaching. He made to cut him, but to his surprise Mr. Berkeley hailed him like an old friend.

"Good day to you, Bergrave," said Mr. Berkeley cheerfully. "As you can see, my poor face is still a mess."

"You deserved more," said Lord Andrew coldly.

Mr. Berkeley spread his hands in a rueful gesture. "I deserved hanging."

Lord Andrew frowned. "We would have had that fellow you hired hanging outside Newgate if there had not been a need to avoid scandal. It is you who are the murderer anyway."

"I did not hire him to kill Digby," said Mr. Berkeley. "His instructions were to fire over Digby's head and put him off his aim. I was going to fire in the air. I could not see any point in one of us taking the life of another over such as Miss Wraxall."

"Be careful what you say of that lady, sir," raged Lord Andrew.

"I say nothing wrong. She drove me mad," said Mr. Berkeley. "But only consider, would you not agree that she is a flirt? Even you must have noticed how she led me on."

Lord Andrew had, in fact, been very angry at the way Delilah had so openly flirted with Mr. Berkeley. And she had flirted with *him*!

"Miss Wraxall is now Digby's concern," he said. "They are to be married. Digby has gone to ask Mr. Wraxall for his consent."

"I wish him all happiness." Mr. Berkeley looked steadily at Lord Andrew. "I behaved disgracefully, I admit, but she drove me to the point of insanity. We all wondered why her father should find it necessary to place her in the Tribbles' care, but now we know. Delilah Wraxall is dangerous. I am glad Digby will now have the schooling of her."

"Then there is nothing further to say." Lord Andrew nodded curtly and walked on.

Mr. Berkeley stood for a few moments watching him go, his mind racing. So Digby was out of Town. Mr. Berkeley thirsted for revenge. He took himself off to a coffee-house to plot and plan.

132

"What is all that rumpus?" demanded Sir Charles crossly. He was preparing to set out for London again. He had gained the squire's permission and had got him to agree to a wedding in a fortnight's time. He was anxious to return to London to make arrangements to bring Delilah home.

"It's Jane, one of the scullery maids," said his butler.

"Why is she weeping and wailing like that?" demanded Sir Charles.

"She is with child," said the butler.

"Then get the father here to me before I leave so I may constrain him to marry the girl."

"I am afraid the father is a strolling chapman she met at the fair last summer. We cannot find him now."

Sir Charles made a noise of impatience and went out into the hall.

Jane, the scullery maid, was standing there with a small basket at her feet. Her eyes were swollen with crying and she was a most unlovely sight.

"Stop blubbering," snapped Sir Charles. "How came you to get in this state?"

"H-he s-said he l-loved me and would m-marry me," said poor Jane and fell to crying harder than ever.

Sir Charles fished in his pocket. He was about to hand the girl a couple of guineas and send her on her way, but as he looked at her, her weeping face under the squashed straw-bonnet was replaced by that of Delilah, a Delilah whose voice sounded in his ears, saying, "What will become of her?"

"Have you any family?" asked Sir Charles gently.

It took her some time to answer, but at last she said, "No, sir. Got me from the orphanage."

Sir Charles sighed. He said to his butler, "I shall not be leaving yet. I must call on the squire and the vicar again and see if we cannot find a husband for this poor girl." He was sure Delilah would understand and think he had done just as he ought.

The Tribbles were in a high state of excitement. Delilah was to be married and they already had a client to replace her. A letter had arrived that morning summoning them to an address in Croydon. A Mr. and Mrs. Perry-Sommers wished to engage their services as soon as possible. Money was no object.

On the following day after the letter arrived, Amy and Effy set out, telling Delilah to study her piano scales and keep a close watch on Yvette.

Delilah saw them off and decided to spend the day reading instead. Yvette had come up from the depths of despair and was so filled with gratitude for the Tribbles that it was unlilkely she would do anything silly.

Then Harris, the butler, came in, looking excited. He said he had received a letter from the Three Tuns Tavern to say that Miss Amy Tribble had arranged a special luncheon for all the servants.

Delilah was torn between amusement and exasperation. "How like Amy," she said, "to forget to tell me. Yes, Harris. You may all go. I shall do very well on my own."

What an odd pair the sisters were, thought Delilah as she listened to all the excitement and bustle as the servants made their way out to enjoy this unexpected treat. Who else in London society would think of giving all their servants a luncheon? She decided to tell her father to present the sisters with some extra money. She knew

Amy and Effy were constantly worried about their finances.

The house fell silent. The day outside was grey and cold and the lowering sky threatened snow.

Delilah was completely alone, and alone with her thoughts. She tried to tell herself she loved Sir Charles and that she had nothing to fear, and yet, as the minutes ticked by, she found she could not remember him very clearly or the passion he had aroused in her body.

A hammering on the street door roused her from her uneasy reverie. Callers, she thought, and was glad of the interruption. How odd whoever it was would think it to find her alone!

She ran lightly down the stairs and opened the door. Mr. Guy Berkeley stood on the doorstep. Delilah made to slam the door, but he put his foot in it.

"Hear me out, Miss Wraxall," he begged. "I am come to offer my most humble apology."

"Your apology is accepted," said Delilah curtly, pushing ineffectually at the door.

"You must hear me out," he pleaded. "I am leaving England forever, but I cannot go without giving you an explanation of what happened."

"Well . . ." Delilah hesitated.

"Lady, had it not been for your flirtation with me, for the fact that you roused false hopes in my bosom," said Mr. Berkeley, "then I never would have behaved so disgracefully. Pray, grant me an audience."

Delilah remembered her own behaviour and her face turned pink. She had indeed led him on disgracefully and all to get revenge on Sir Charles.

"But you hired a murderer to kill Sir Charles," she protested.

"I swear on my oath that the silly fellow was not hired

135

to murder Sir Charles. He was told to fire over Digby's head to startle him and throw him off his aim while I fired in the air. Madam, I am a friend of the Prince Regent, I am a respectable member of the ton, I am not a murderer. Please allow me just a few moments."

Delilah opened the door. "Just a little," she said crossly, "but I really do not know what else there is to say."

She led the way up to the drawing-room. "I should not be doing this," she said. She was about to tell him she was alone in the house and then decided against it.

She walked into the drawing-room and sat down on the sofa.

"Now, sir," said Delilah, "say what you have to say and please leave."

"You are alone?" he asked. "The servants have left?"

"Yes," said Delilah, and then her eyes widened in alarm. Everything rushed into her brain at once—the unexpected letter summoning the Tribbles, the unexpected lunch for the servants, and the rather nasty look which had appeared in Mr. Berkeley's eyes.

"I have changed my mind," she said breathlessly, rising to her feet. "Go now. I do not want to hear what you have to say."

She made to walk past him to the door, but he drew back his arm and struck her hard on the side of the head. Delilah fell heavily on the floor and he landed on top of her with such force that he drove the breath out of her body. His hands tore at her gown. "Jade," he said thickly. "I'll teach you to make a fool of me."

He forced his mouth down on hers and drove his tongue between her lips. She bit his tongue hard and when he swore and freed her mouth she screamed with all her might.

Upstairs in her room, Yvette, who had not gone with

136

the other servants, heard that scream. Miss Wraxall! Miss Wraxall must have screamed. And she, Yvette, had heard the sound of a man's voice a few moments earlier. Delilah screamed again.

Yvette had been mending Amy's stays. One of the whalebones in her Apollo corset had come unfastened from its moorings and Amy had complained that the end of the stay had broken off so that it had been digging into her like a spear. Yvette had just been in the process of sewing in a new stay. The old one, with the sharp broken end, lay discarded on the work-table beside her.

She seized it in her hand and left her room and began to creep down the stairs.

Delilah's head was reeling from all the punches Mr. Berkeley had rained on it. Her skirts were dragged up and his hand was fumbling between her legs. She jerked her knee up sharply and caught him in a tender place and he brought both hands up round her throat and began to squeeze hard.

Yvette moved quickly into the drawing-room and saw the man lying on top of Delilah, saw his hands around her throat. She raised the whalebone stay like a dagger and brought it down with the force of a madwoman right into the back of Guy Berkeley's neck.

He let out a terrible animal scream. His eyes bulged in his head. He rolled off Delilah and lay on his side, the stay sticking out of the back of his neck.

Weeping and cursing, Yvette pulled the stay out and a fountain of blood spurted over her gown.

She pulled Delilah to her feet, ineffectually trying to hold the front of her torn gown together for her.

Delilah swayed on her feet and grabbed hold of a chair back to support herself.

"Never mind me," she gasped. "Get a surgeon."

"For that *canaille*?" said Yvette, giving the body a contemptuous kick with her foot. "He is dead."

Delilah dropped to her knees and felt feverishly for Mr. Berkeley's pulse. There was not even a flutter of life. Delilah bent her head and began to cry.

"Do not weep," said Yvette, crouching down beside her and holding her tight. "He would have raped you, killed you. It is better this way."

Amy and Effy returned tired and cross. There had been no such address in Croydon and no such people. They had made inquiries all over the town before coming to the conclusion they had been gulled and had passed the bitter time on the journey back by speculating as to which of their jealous society friends would have paid such a trick on them.

They entered the house and straight into chaos. The servants were screaming and yelling. There was what appeared to be a whole regiment of the militia, two Bow Street Runners, two physicians, four gentlemen of the press, and Mr. Haddon, standing in the hall, trying to stop the babble, his face like clay.

"Silence!" roared Amy. "Mr. Haddon, what is going on. Delilah . . . ?"

"Miss Wraxall is safe," he said. "Mr. Berkeley lured the servants away from the house and then tried to rape Miss Wraxall."

"I'll kill him," said Amy.

"He has already been killed," said Mr. Haddon quietly. "By Yvette. She fortunately did not go with the others and heard Miss Wraxall scream."

Effy swayed against Mr. Haddon and he caught her around the waist.

Despite her horror and confusion, Amy dragged Effy out of Mr. Haddon's arms and thrust her at Baxter, saying brutally, "Pull yourself together, Effy. Now is not the time to be missish."

Shouting, ordering and commanding, Amy sent the servants off to their duties, collected the officers of the law together and marched them into the library. She showed them the letter, saying she had no doubt now the handwriting would prove to be that of Mr. Berkeley. They had arrested Yvette, and Amy howled at them to unarrest her immediately or she would make them look like the biggest fools in Christendom. She became angrier and angrier and more and more overwrought until Mr. Haddon stepped in and took command.

Amy fell silent and sat with her face buried in her hands while Mr. Haddon competently set about dealing with the whole mess.

The village of Hoppleton received the London newspapers a day late. The squire settled down to read two of them beside a roaring fire. A blizzard was blowing outside, and he felt warm and snug.

He carefully read all the advertisements on the front before turning to the inside pages. The murder of Mr. Guy Berkeley did not interest him. He had never heard of the fellow. He read the social notes and the foreign news. He was about to toss the paper aside and reach for another one when the sight of the name Wraxall caught his eye. He carefully read the details of the murder of Mr. Guy Berkeley and felt himself grow as cold as the day outside.

Sir Charles Digby erupted into the room. "I must leave immediately," he said. "Have you read the news?"

"This is dreadful," whispered the squire. "Why did I

ever let her go to that beastly city?" He shouted to his servants to get his travelling carriage ready.

"No need for that," said Sir Charles. "Mine is ready outside. We can travel together."

They drove only two miles out of Hoppleton in the blinding snowstorm when their carriage ended up in the ditch with the pole broken, the luggage scattered in the snow, and the terrified horses rearing and plunging. The squire was knocked unconscious and the coachman had a broken arm. Sir Charles and his two grooms laboured to get the squire's unconscious body over the saddle of one of the horses, and, leading the horse, Sir Charles set out back to the village, worried out of his mind about Delilah.

The snowstorm raged over London, covering the sooty city in a white blanket, silencing the streets, making the great metropolis appear as dead and as lifeless as it had been during the Great Plague.

Delilah recovered quickly physically, but mentally she felt very low. She had promised to marry Sir Charles and now she felt she could not bear to see him or any other man again.

While the snow continued to fall, there was nothing that could be done. Amy and Effy had to consult their lawyers to make sure no blame would stick to Yvette. There were no callers, apart from Mr. Haddon, who had arrived just before the full force of the storm and was now resident in Holles Street, as he was unable to get home.

The knocker was tied up, a sign to the press and the curious that the Tribbles were not receiving any visitors at all.

Amy was sick with worry, but she kept her worries to

herself. It was hard to tell whether Effy was acting weak and distressed in order to arouse Mr. Haddon's manly sympathies or whether she was really upset. But she looked so scared and frail that Amy could not bring herself to add to her sister's worries.

Delilah, who had been very quiet and serious since the attempted rape, finally sought out Amy and told her quietly that there was to be no marriage. She, Delilah, would return home to Hoppleton as soon as the roads were cleared.

Amy's cup of bitterness was full.

"I am sure your father and Sir Charles will soon be with us," she said. "They will have read the newspapers, but there is no way they can reach us in such conditions."

Amy had meant to keep all her fears to herself, but that evening, after Delilah had retired, Amy watched Mr. Haddon and Effy with a sour expression. Mr. Haddon had a skein of brightly coloured wool stretched between his hands and Effy was winding it into a ball.

"We look quite like an old married couple, do we not?" called Effy gaily.

Amy's temper snapped. "I held my peace while you looked as frightened and worried as I, Effy," she raged. "But now I see you must have been play-acting as usual. Here we are in a terrible, dreadful mess and you sit there, like some old harpy, flirting and ogling without a care in the world."

Effy stole a look at Mr. Haddon. "Can it be that Amy is jealous?" she murmured.

Amy heard that murmur. She got to her feet and tore the skein of wool out of Mr. Haddon's hands and threw it on the floor.

"Are you deaf and blind as well as dumb?" she shouted at Effy. "Do you not know what has happened?"

"Oh, sit down, do," said Effy crossly. "It is no use ranting and raving and trying to get me worked up, Amy. It has all been quite awful, to be sure, but as soon as the snow stops, we will turn the matter over to our lawyers and that will be the end of it."

"You really don't know," said Amy, amazed. "Let me spell it out for you: We earn our living sponsoring young girls and finding them husbands. There has been an attempted rape in this house and a murder while we were gulled into travelling to Croydon. Who, in the name of a demi-rep's disease-ridden bum is going to send anyone to us now?"

Effy looked stricken. "B-but, perhaps it is not so very bad. We have had two successes already and now we have a third."

"No, we haven't," said Amy. "Delilah ain't going to marry Sir Charles, and that's that."

Effy began to cry and Mr. Haddon looked at Amy reproachfully.

"It's no use looking at me like that," said Amy. "She's got to see sense. Think, Mr. Haddon! Is anyone in their right mind going to send a daughter to us now?"

And Mr. Haddon slowly shook his head.

Chapter 8

The slavery of the tea and coffee and other slop-kettle

William Cobbett

T HE SISTERS WERE UNAWARE that in a quiet and fashionable street in Bath, events were taking place which would bring them another customer.

Viscount and Viscountess Clarendon had arranged a tea-party. The purpose of this sedate affair was to introduce their daughter, the Honourable Clarissa Vevian, to a prospective suitor. They felt it was their last hope. Mr. Paul Deveney had but lately come to Bath. New blood might be luckier than old.

It was not that Clarissa was in any way repulsive in appearance. It was simply that she was infernally clumsy.

And dangerously so.

She had broken a bone in a gentleman's foot only the other week at an assembly by landing on it enthusiastically from a great height after completing an entrechat in the quadrille. Clarissa had tearfully pointed out that the gentleman should not have been in the way when she came down to land.

Lord Fremney had been playing a tune to her on the piano and Clarissa had somehow forgotten he was there or even that he was playing and had slammed down the lid of the piano and had broken his fingers. She seemed to have cut a swath of disaster through Bath.

She had received written instructions from her mother as to how to go on at the tea-party. She was to sit, unmoving, and let her mother pour the tea and hand round the cakes. She was not to move at all. Not a muscle.

Her maid, Jessop, had been given so many instructions as to how best to prettify her young mistress that she had overfussed and primped until Clarissa's head felt as if it were on fire from all the crimping and singeing and curling.

The Honourable Clarissa was a tall girl, very tall, and walked with a stoop. Her hair was dark red, a sad defect, and her eyes, her finest feature, were of a clear grey. She had large, well-shaped feet, but large feet were considered a common-looking disgrace and she was constantly being constrained to wear shoes too small for her, and so she walked with a shuffling gait and a pained look on her face. And with the white-lead cosmetic her parents made her wear, she often looked like a weird apparition.

Half an hour before the "last hope" was due to arrive for tea, Lord and Lady Clarendon again studied an old newspaper, which carried the Tribbles' advertisement.

"Well, that's out now," sighed Lord Clarendon. "Murder, indeed!"

"But there are so many wickednesses in the world," said his wife, "and I know Effy Tribble. She is a sweet creature and very bon ton. Don't you think . . . ?"

The viscount shook his head. "Can't send our only daughter into a household where there's been a murder. I have great hopes of Deveney. I have been told he could do with some money and Clarissa has a very good dowry. As long as she remembers not to move, she will do very well."

Clarissa was seated in the drawing-room behind the tea-table at four o'clock, the time Mr. Deveney was due to arrive. She felt ugly and miserable. Her hair, from over-frizzing and -curling, looked lifeless. She felt slightly unwell and seemed to have no energy whatsoever. She was sure that the blanc that covered her face, neck and arms was giving her cosmetic poisoning, a common-enough complaint, but one neither her parents nor her maid appeared to have heard of.

Her mother sat at the other side of the tea-table, a small, delicate creature with hair as fine and silvery as Effy Tribble's. The viscount sat a little way away on Clarissa's other side. He too was small in stature, but slim and elegant and dressed in his finest.

The large Clarissa sat between them like a miserable cuckoo chick.

"Mr. Paul Deveney," announced the butler.

Clarissa made to rise but her mother frowned a warning at her and went forward herself to greet Mr. Deveney. He was a small Exquisite, dressed in the latest of wasp-waisted fashions and with very high heels to his boots and fixed spurs. His face was stained with walnut juice and the palms of his hands were dyed pink with cochineal. He carried a clouded cane in one hand and a highly scented handkerchief in the other.

He sat at the tea-table and discoursed at length on the provincialism of Bath society. The Clarendons politely agreed, glancing nervously at their large daughter to make sure she did not move.

And then all hell broke out from somewhere downstairs. There were screams and crashes and calls for help.

The viscount ran to the door and could shortly be heard calling down from the landing, asking what the fuss was about.

"Lady Howard's horse ran away with her and her carriage is splintered against our railings, my lord," came the reply.

The viscountess rose to her feet in great agitation. "Pray excuse me, Mr. Deveney," she said. "Lady Howard is my oldest friend."

She fled from the room. There was a short silence during which Mr. Deveney looked at Clarissa and Clarissa looked into the middle distance. Clarissa would have liked to go and look out of the window at the accident but had promised not to move, and Mr. Deveney had no interest in anyone else's welfare other than his own.

"I would like some more tea," said Mr. Deveney at last.

"Of course," Clarissa picked up the teapot and found it empty. Well, she would have to rise to get more. No point in ringing for the servants when they were all busy at the accident. She carried it over to a silver urn on the sideboard where the water was being kept at a low boil over a spirit-stove.

Poor Clarissa. Her feet hurt and her head hurt and she felt large and stupid and ugly in front of the dainty little Mr. Deveney, who was watching her with a certain rather waspish amusement in his eyes.

In fact, he *is* like a wasp, thought Clarissa, with that ridiculously nipped-in coat and that black-and-gold-striped waistcoat. People like Mr. Deveney should be swatted; nasty, buzzing, spiteful creature. She made a flapping motion with her hand as if swiping a wasp and knocked the urn and spirit-stove flying. Clarissa leapt back with a scream as a Niagara of boiling water cascaded across the floor.

Mr. Deveney tried to leap up but his spurs got entangled with each other and he fell under the table. The spirit-stove had rolled under the table and had set the pretty lace cover alight.

"The table-cloth's on fire," shouted Mr. Deveney, wriggling out from under the table like an eel.

Clarissa seized the burning table-cloth, sending cakes and cups and dishes flying, and threw it over in the direction of the window; then she kicked the spirit-stove across the room. The table-cloth set the curtains alight and the trail of spirits from the stove sent the carpet up in flames.

As Clarissa tugged at the bell-rope for help and then tried to stamp out the flames, Mr. Deveney, who still had hopes of Clarissa's dowry, caught her round the waist and cried, "I shall save you."

"I don't need saving," said Clarissa crossly. She gave him what she considered a gentle shove, but he went flying backwards into the flaming curtains. His hair went up like a torch and he tore it off, revealing it had been only a wig and that he was as bald as a coot underneath.

Clarissa obligingly jumped up and down on his wig to put the flames out as the servants came running in with pails of water.

Lord and Lady Clarendon came into the wreck of their once pretty drawing-room to find Mr. Deveney a sobbing, demoralized creature and their daughter trying to comfort him by putting a charred wig on his head.

Both agreed later that that was the very moment when they decided to send Clarissa to the Tribbles.

Unaware of the good fortune about to descend on them, Effy and Amy Tribble, once the thaw came, coped competently with lawyers and burst pipes alike.

The genius of McAdam had not stretched as far as the village of Hoppleton, and when Sir Charles finally set out, he had to struggle through miles of mud and flooded rivers on foot before reaching a good posting-house where he could hire a horse and find a decent road leading to London to ride it on. He had not taken any servants with him, preferring to face the rigours of the journey alone. A husband in the person of a farm labourer had been found for the scullery maid and a vacant cottage on Sir Charles's estate had been refurbished for the couple. He was looking forward to telling Delilah all about it. She would learn that he was not hard and unfeeling.

The squire was still confined to bed, recovering from his accident. Sir Charles had not learned of Delilah's change of heart, for the post-boy had been unable to reach the village, and the squire had begged Sir Charles to bring Delilah home.

He finally was on his way on horseback for London, relishing the change in the weather. The sky above was a pale washed-out blue and a mist was rising from the sodden fields.

Sir Charles was sure Delilah would be delighted not only to see him but to escape from that dreadful house. He rode straight to Holles Street. It was the middle of the afternoon when he arrived, and he found to his irritation that the ladies had gone out on calls.

He felt he ought to find a hotel and change out of his

muddy clothes, but the desire to see Delilah was so great that he told the butler, Harris, that he would wait. He expected the Tribble sisters to be thoroughly ashamed of themselves. He wondered who was receiving them, for surely the shame of failing to protect their charge had put them beyond the social pale.

But it was thanks to Delilah that the Tribble sisters were now the most sought-after ladies in Town. Having become fond of them and knowing how badly they had been tricked by Mr. Berkeley, Delilah had become expert at telling her story very dramatically. One hostess told another, and Delilah and the Tribbles were soon heavily in demand, everyone wanting to hear first-hand of Delilah's Gothic adventure.

Sir Charles heard their return and the chatter of voices in the hall downstairs, followed by a sudden silence. Then, to his horror, he heard Miss Amy say clearly, "We shall explain matters if you like, Delilah. You have been through so much. We would not want to cause you any more pain."

Delilah answered something in a low voice that he could not hear.

He rose to his feet as they entered the room. Delilah was looking bewitching in a morning dress of black bombazine covered with a short mantle of silver cloth.

She turned to the sisters and said quietly, "I shall see Sir Charles alone."

Effy made to protest, but Amy pulled her from the room.

Delilah unpinned her bonnet and placed it on a side-table and then turned to Sir Charles.

"How is my father?" she asked.

"I am afraid he is not well yet," said Sir Charles. "Of course, you do not know. We set out some time ago for

London, but the carriage overturned in the ditch and Mr. Wraxall was knocked unconscious. He is recovering fast with Mrs. Cavendish to tend him. I told him I would ride to London and bring you home."

"Of course I shall go as soon as possible," said Delilah. "Poor Papa. Are you sure he is better?"

"Much better. Mrs. Cavendish is an excellent nurse. I have made arrangements with the vicar to marry us as soon as we return. Mr. Wraxall says it would be fine to have a double wedding, so he will be marrying Mrs. Cavendish at the same time. What is the matter? You are very pale. Your father is not in any danger."

Delilah looked at him sadly. "I am trying to find the courage to tell you I cannot marry you."

Sir Charles took an angry step towards her and she backed away, holding up one hand. "Do not come near me, sir," she said. "I cannot be forced to marry when I don't want to."

"You jade," he raged. "Once a heart-breaker, always a heart-breaker. You led me on. Was it revenge you wanted? I feel like shaking you."

He took another threatening step forward. Amy appeared in the doorway.

"Go to your room, Delilah," she said. "I will handle matters here."

Amy waited until Delilah had left, and said, "That is no way to speak to her."

"How else do you expect me to speak to her?" said Sir Charles. "Is this a result of your schooling? She is a worse flirt than ever she was!"

"Sit down, Sir Charles," said Amy wearily. "Now you must realize Delilah has had a very nasty experience. Very nasty. It is not you she dislikes at the moment, she is simply afraid of all men. If your courtship had not been so forward, she might perhaps be less afraid of you. If you want to win her back, then I suggest you begin to woo her properly and patiently."

"And what do you, a spinster, know of such matters?"

Amy looked like a whipped horse, and Sir Charles said quickly, "Forgive me. I did not mean that. But you must see how it looks from my point of view."

"I can understand your point of view," said Amy. "Now try to understand Delilah's. She was badly beaten by Mr. Berkeley and nearly raped. She may believe that is how all men are. I know you want to shout at her and give her a good shaking, but if you still want her, then that is not the way to go about it."

"Do you not think I, too, have sometimes had doubts about this marriage?" said Sir Charles. "I was sometimes afraid that she would turn from a flighty girl into a flighty matron. But the love I had for her was so strong, I was prepared to take that risk. I can see now that I have had a lucky escape."

Amy sighed. "And I can see your pride is badly hurt. Are you come to take her home?"

"Yes. Mr. Wraxall was knocked unconscious in a carriage accident. Mrs. Cavendish is nursing him and he is recovering fast, but he is anxious to have his daughter back home."

"Then it is as well she goes," said Amy sadly. "You cannot travel alone with her in a closed carriage. Effy and I will go with you. It is the least we can do for Delilah. I have an account with the livery stables. We can set out in two days' time."

"Why not earlier?"

A ghost of a smile played on Amy's lips. "Because it will take some time to persuade my sister to face the evils of the countryside. Please think of what I have said, Sir

151

Charles. Delilah is a warm and generous woman, a woman any man should be proud to court and woo. All it takes is a little patience."

"I shall call for her in two days' time," said Sir Charles stiffly. "Your servant, ma'am."

"Absolutely ridiculous," raged Effy when she heard the plan. "You know how I detest the country, Amy. Bad smelly drains and bad smelly peasants. Besides, Mr. Haddon is to take us to the playhouse."

"Look, Effy." Amy sat down and glared at her sister. "You are forgetting about our job, and that job is to find a husband for Delilah. She loves him and he loves her, but there's fright on the one hand and pride on the other. We should see it through. Thanks to Delilah, our reputation is much restored. Now if only we could get her married, I feel we would be back in business again."

In vain did Effy protest; Amy was adamant. Effy had made up her mind to pretend to fall ill when a letter arrived from Mr. Haddon to say he was suffering from the ague and would be unable to escort them to the play. Effy thought of being left alone in the house, for she did not consider the servants as company, expecting every moment that another mad rapist would come bounding up the stairs. At last, she set her mind to travel to the dreaded country, deciding to wear a pair of smoked glasses so that she should not have to look too closely at the place.

When they finally set out, the mercurial English weather had changed again. The sky was leaden and a biting wind blew from the north-east. Effy, Amy, Delilah, and the maid, Baxter, travelled inside the coach and Sir Charles rode alongside.

Delilah had feared he would renew his attentions, but

he was polite and chilly and distant and she consoled herself with the thought that she was better off not being married to such an icy mortal.

But she could not help glancing out of the carriage window at him. He rode easily and well. A cheeky housemaid, shaking a rug out of an upstairs window, blew Sir Charles a kiss and he smiled and raised his hat.

If that girl were in my employ, thought Delilah, I would send her packing. She took out a book and began to read.

When she looked up again, it was to see small flakes of snow beginning to blow outside the carriage.

"What weather!" said Amy with a shiver. She pulled down the window and called to Sir Charles, "How far to the nearest town?"

"About ten miles, I think," he called back. The snow fell heavier and heavier. The wind had dropped, but great flakes blanketed the landscape. Soon, Sir Charles looked like a snowman on horseback.

Amy leaned out of the window again. "Tie your horse on behind," she called, "and travel inside with us."

"Madam," came Sir Charles's voice, "I can assure you it is much warmer out here."

"Which means he is still in a huff," said Amy, slamming up the window. "Are you quite sure you cannot bear the idea of him, Delilah?"

"We have been through all that before," said Delilah, barricading herself behind her book.

The coach creaked forward, becoming slower and slower.

"I can't see a thing," said Effy, wiping the glass with her sleeve.

"Then take those dark glasses off," snapped Amy. "You look like a guy."

"I've heard there are highwaymen in these parts, mum," said Baxter with a shiver.

Suddenly they were surrounded by lights and noise. Amy seized the window-strap and lowered the window. They had rolled into the courtyard of an inn.

"Praise be to God," said Baxter fervently.

The ladder was let down and the ladies alighted from the coach. Sir Charles had dismounted and was shouting orders to the ostlers.

"Go into the inn," he called. "I shall join you directly."

They made their way into an old-fashioned hall where the carcasses of game and legs of mutton hung from the ceiling.

Soon Sir Charles joined them and summoned the landlord. They all went up to their rooms, agreeing to meet in the dining-hall as soon as they had washed and changed.

When they entered the dining-hall half an hour later, it was to find they were not the only stranded passengers. The long tables were full of people.

It was a silent meal. Sir Charles was stiff and formal and icily polite and Delilah picked at her food and seemed on the point of tears. Well, what did she expect? thought Amy desperately. Doesn't she realize she's jilted the man?

Then Amy's gaze softened as she looked at Delilah. Delilah had all the beauty that Amy herself had always longed to have. This stubborn pair, Sir Charles and Delilah, Amy thought, would probably go off and marry other people and be totally miserable. Amy drew the other guests at the table into conversation, but most of them were young men who seemed dazzled with Delilah, which made Sir Charles frostier than ever.

At last the meal was over and they could retire to their rooms. But it was still snowing hard and there seemed little hope they could set out in the morning.

Effy was sharing a bedchamber with Delilah, and Baxter had a truckle-bed set up in the corner of Amy's room.

Despite her misery, Delilah was amused by Effy's preparations for bed. Effy carefully wound her silver hair into curl papers, then she slapped her face vigorously with cream before tying a chin-strap tightly about her head.

"Do you mind if I read for a little?" asked Delilah.

"If you must," said Effy huffily. "I shall put on my dark glasses to protect my eyes from the light."

Delilah settled back against the pillows, opened a romance, and began to read.

It was a Gothic romance in which an Italian countess was locked in a haunted room in an old castle in Tuscany. In the book, Delilah had just reached the bit where the heroine was trying to persuade herself that the ghost of the murdered princess did not exist when a loud and eerie wail came from behind the tapestry. The description was so vivid that Delilah thought she had actually heard that sinister cry. "Get thee to Hell, or get thee to Heaven, but do not plague me, restless spirit," cried the heroine. Another eerie wail.

Delilah put down her book and frowned. That wail had not been her imagination. Then, from next door, she heard Baxter cry out.

Delilah climbed out of bed and pulled on a wrapper and went next door.

"It's Miss Amy!" cried Baxter. "She do be mortal sick."

Delilah nervously approached the bed. Amy stared at her with feverish, dilated eyes. "Who are you?" she said faintly.

"It is I, Delilah." Delilah sat down by the bed and took Amy's large hand in her own. She looked up at Baxter. "You must fetch Sir Charles and tell him to find a physician. And get Miss Effy."

Soon Sir Charles and Effy were standing by the bed.

Effy began to cry, wringing her hands, and moaning, "Oh, my poor sister."

"I shall go and search for a physician," said Sir Charles quietly.

Amy appeared to fall into a restless sleep. Effy, Baxter and Delilah sat by the fire, waiting and worrying. After an hour, Sir Charles entered the room with a small, elderly man.

"Mr. Mackay will take a look at Miss Amy," he said. "I suggest we all wait outside."

They stood out in the corridor. Effy was leaning against Baxter for support, her lips moving in prayer. They waited and waited for what seemed like a very long time. Then the doctor came out, shaking his head.

"Miss Tribble has caught a deathly chill," he said. "I have attended many such cases in this town and they all died."

Effy let out a cry and fainted dead away.

"Carry her to her bed," said Delilah to Baxter. "I shall sit up with Miss Amy. Tell me, Doctor, is there anything I can do?"

The doctor shook his head mournfully. "Very little now," he said. "I have bled her. Bathe her temples with cologne and keep the fire made up. She may surprise you by being very hungry. They are like that in the final stages. Give her any food she wants. I shall call again in the morning."

Delilah's voice trembled. "Is there no hope?"

"You can pray," said the doctor, making his way to the stairs.

Delilah slowly entered the room. Sir Charles followed her.

Amy, with a face like clay, lay against the pillows. She

was snoring horribly and her nightcap was tipped over one eye. Delilah gently straightened it and sat down by the bed. Sir Charles built up the fire and carried a chair over to sit with Delilah.

"She *must* live," whispered Delilah. "She is always so strong, so well. I had come to love her."

"There is always hope," said Sir Charles gently. He smiled ruefully at Delilah. "You are having a miserable time."

"None of that matters," said Delilah fiercely. "If only she would recover."

"We will stay here and nurse her until she does," he said firmly.

"Are you sure my father is well?" whispered Delilah. "Somehow, Miss Amy's illness has made me fear for him."

"Mr. Wraxall will probably be restored to health by the time you return," said Sir Charles. "Let us call a truce, Delilah. We are not to be married, but we can be comfortable together while we care for Miss Amy."

His voice was gentle and kind and his smile sweet. Delilah felt all those old treacherous stirrings in her body that she had almost forgotten.

"Very well," she said in a stifled voice. "Truce it is."

"My hand on it." Delilah took his hand and then dropped it abruptly as if she had been burnt. She muttered an excuse and went to her own room to change into a warm gown. Baxter was holding Effy, who had fallen asleep. Delilah returned to Sir Charles. They sat quietly together, taking comfort from each other's presence as the hours slowly passed.

"While Miss Amy sleeps, I may as well give you the gossip of Hoppleton," said Sir Charles. He began to talk softly while Delilah listened and watched his face in the firelight. "And you will not think me too bad a fellow," he ended, "when I tell you that one of my scullery maids was with child and I managed to find a husband for her before I left."

"You found a husband for her? How?"

"One of the farm labourers was only too happy to wed her in return for a cottage and some money."

"Could you not find the real father?"

"No. He was a travelling chapman."

"But does the girl *like* this labourer she is being constrained to marry?" asked Delilah.

"That does not enter into it," said Sir Charles. "Yes, she is delighted not to be turned out into the street."

"But why should she be turned out into the street for something that was not really her fault?"

"I cannot persuade myself the girl was entirely blameless," said Sir Charles dryly.

"No, of course you can't," said Delilah. "You must always blame the woman, must you not? I—"

Amy groaned and shifted in the bed. Then she sat bolt upright and stared at the bedpost. "Oh, bright angel," she cried. "You are come to take me home!"

"Shhh," said Delilah, pressing her back against the pillows. "There is no angel there. Oh, Charles, help me. I cannot bear this."

He put a hand on Amy's brow and said in a deep, quiet voice, "You must rest and grow strong, Miss Amy."

Amy appeared to lose consciousness. But her breath was rapid and shallow.

Sir Charles sighed. "You had best fetch Miss Effy, Delilah."

Soon they were all clustered about the bed. A red dawn crept into the room. Amy tossed and muttered and then said feebly, "Effy, are you there?"

158

"Oh, yes, sister dear," whispered Effy. "Don't leave me, Amy. Please don't leave me."

Amy's eyes opened. "I am going to a far country where there is no pain, no suffering," she said in a hollow voice. Tears were streaming down Delilah's cheeks. Sir Charles gathered her in his arms and she leaned her head against his chest. Baxter fell to her knees at the foot of the bed and began to pray.

"My last dying wish," said Amy faintly, "is that Sir Charles and Delilah will marry."

"Please tell her you will," cried Effy.

Sir Charles looked down into Delilah's eyes. "We are a pair of fools, are we not? I love you with all my heart and soul, Delilah Wraxall. Will you marry me?"

"Oh, yes," said Delilah. "I love you, too, Charles."

Amy sat up straight and raised her hands to heaven. "My blessing on you both," she said. "Now I can go to my grave with a clear conscience."

Effy flung herself across her sister's body. "I shall be all alone," she sobbed. "There is no one but you, Amy. I cannot live without you."

Sir Charles raised Baxter to her feet. "Go to Miss Effy and comfort her," he said. Amy had slumped back against the pillows. Sir Charles tenderly smoothed Amy's hair back from her brow. There was a great lump in his throat. Overcome with emotion, he went and stood by the window and stared miserably down into the snow-covered whiteness of the inn yard.

He raised his hand and leaned it against the glass. Delilah came to stand beside him and he took his hand away from the cold window-pane and put it at her waist. "Do not worry, Delilah," he said. "The end cannot be far now. I shall go and find the physician and see if he can give me some drug to alleviate her pain."

Delilah leaned against him, weeping softly.

Sir Charles looked bleakly at the window and then saw that his hand had left a white imprint on the glass. He drew his hand gently from Delilah's waist and looked at it. It was smeared with white. Then he looked at Amy's clay-coloured face.

"Delilah," he said in a low voice. "Stay here. I am going to find that physician."

Mr. Mackay was tucking into a breakfast of York ham, cold pheasant, game pie, lamb chops, devilled kidneys and curried eggs, all washed down with old ale, when Sir Charles strode into his parlour.

"My dear Sir Charles," said the physician. "I am just having a light repast before calling on Miss Tribble. Has she survived the night?"

"Yes," said Sir Charles, sitting down at the table, "and like to survive a good many more. How much did she pay you?"

"I do not know what you mean. Miss Amy Tribble is at death's door."

"If Miss Amy Tribble is going to die of anything, it might be from lead poisoning," said Sir Charles. "She must have about one inch of blanc on her face."

"Indeed!" The physician shook his head. "Ah, the ladies. Exhausted after the journey and already ill, she must have forgot to remove her cosmetic."

"I do not know what she paid you," said Sir Charles evenly, "but I will pay double for the truth."

Mr. Mackay, a little Scotchman with sandy hair and bristling eyebrows, looked thoughtfully at his plate and then speared a kidney and popped it into his mouth. Then he dabbed his mouth with his napkin and said, "Five guineas."

"Then I shall give you ten," said Sir Charles. "You will

make me up the nastiest concoction you can think of. I shall tell Miss Amy it is a new miracle medicine. Do you understand me?"

Mr. Mackay grinned. "I understand you very well."

"Then finish your breakfast, make up a bottle of something, and come to the inn with me."

When Sir Charles entered the bedchamber and saw how white and wretched Delilah looked, he nearly seized Miss Amy Tribble by the neck and dragged her from the bed.

But if Delilah knew she had been tricked, then Delilah might change her mind again.

So instead, he said, "Do not cry. I bring hope. Mr. Mackay has been working all night on a recipe. He is sure it will cure Miss Amy. Come, Mr. Mackay. Miss Amy is too weak to sit up. Place a funnel in her mouth and I will pour it into her."

Amy had not heard what he said. She only felt something being placed between her lips.

Sir Charles tipped the whole bottle of evil-smelling and foul-tasting stuff down Amy's throat.

Amy Tribble tore the funnel out of her mouth. "How dare you pour that horse's piss down my throat?" she raged. "Odd's whoresons. Have you no thought for a dying woman?"

"It is a miracle," said Sir Charles. He seized a damp face-cloth from the toilet table and scrubbed Amy's face hard. "Only see how her colour has returned!"

Amy darted one sharp intelligent look at him and closed her eyes. "I feel sick," she said weakly.

"I think we should leave her to sleep now," said Sir Charles quietly. "Dry your tears, ladies, and join me for a hearty breakfast. Mr. Mackay has decided that the best treatment following his wonderful medicine is fasting. A day completely without food will soon put Miss Tribble on her feet again.''

Delilah and Effy begged to stay with Amy, but Sir Charles ushered them out of the room, saying if they wished to help their patient, then they must keep their spirits up with a good breakfast.

Delilah prayed for Amy's recovery, Amy who had been instrumental in bringing her such happiness. She could not believe that she had ever wanted to be free of Sir Charles. The man was all heart! Only look how lively and amused he seemed now that the danger to Amy's life appeared to be over.

It was three days before they could set out on the road again. Effy and Baxter and Delilah could talk of nothing but Mr. Mackay's miracle cure. Amy smiled and agreed the man must be a genius, she had never felt so well in her life.

The merry party finally arrived at the squire's to find that gentleman up and about. Amy was cast down by Mrs. Cavendish's very ordinary appearance. Surely it would have been better if the squire had ignored her for some beauty!

Effy was still shaken by the experiences of the road and pleased to find the squire's mansion elegant and comfortable and Mrs. Cavendish prepared to minister to her every need. The Tribbles agreed to stay for the wedding. Both were enjoying the novelty of being mothered and looked after, and even Amy finally gruffly allowed that the squire was lucky and that Mrs. Cavendish was a Trojan.

The weather had turned frosty and fine and Sir Charles was a constant visitor.

And then one week before the weddings, Mrs. Cavendish invited the ladies of the village to one of her readings. New novels were hard to come by and when one arrived, it was considered the duty of the lucky lady to read it aloud to the others.

The ladies of Hoppleton crowded into the squire's comfortable drawing-room and settled down with their workbaskets as Mrs. Cavendish began to read in her pleasant, mellow voice.

Delilah had been dreaming of her wedding when suddenly she realized that there was something dreadfully familiar about the lines which Mrs. Cavendish had just begun to read as Sir Charles walked into the room.

The old marchioness was lying in her bed, near death. Suddenly, she straightened up and stared at the end of the bed. "Oh, bright angel," she cried. "You are come to take me home. I am going to a far country where there is no pain, no suffering." Elizabeth began to cry and Count Florinda seized her hand. The dying marchioness suddenly looked at them. "Grant my last dying wish," she said. "Say you will marry each other."

Delilah rose and left the room and Sir Charles followed her. She waited until they were both out in the garden and said, "She couldn't . . . she didn't . . ."

Sir Charles put his arms about her waist and held her close. "Would it make any difference now to know that she *did* trick us?"

"No," said Delilah. Then she began to laugh. "Was there ever anyone in the whole world like Amy Tribble?"

He began to kiss her so fiercely that neither of them heard the monstrous crash of china as, indoors, the enraged Effy picked up the tea-tray and threw it straight at her sister's head.

Three weeks later, the Tribble sisters made their way back to London. Effy was still barely speaking to Amy. Amy was wrapped up in her own worries and did not notice. During their stay at the squire's, they had been mothered by Mrs. Cavendish, fed enormous meals, and gone for sedate walks. Even Effy had become almost reconciled to life in the country.

But London was soon to swallow them up—black and dangerous, hard and cruel London. The squire had given them a bonus and, generous as it was, the sisters knew it would need to last them a long time. Soon now, they would need to pay off their servants one by one. The Season would come and the Season would go and no one would want their services. And they would have all the responsibility and cost of caring for Yvette's baby.

Mr. Haddon is rich, thought Amy crossly. By George, I don't think I would give a tart's curse if he did marry Effy. At least we would be set for life.

A greasy drizzle was falling when they alighted at Holles Street. As she made her way up to the drawing-room, Amy was glancing this way and that, making a mental record of what they could sell.

She sat down and pulled off her bonnet and flicked through the pile of post. Invitations to this and invitations to that. "We are still fashionable, Effy," said Amy. "Such a pity our career is in ruins."

"I do not wish to speak to you," sniffed Effy. "Liar and cheat."

"Do not prose on," said Amy. "Here's a letter for you with a crest on it."

Effy fumbled in her bosom for her eyeglass, cracked open the seal and began to read.

"It's from Georgiana, Viscountess Clarendon," said Effy in a wondering voice. "She wants to hire us to school her daughter, Clarissa. 'I do not know your fees, dear Effy,' she writes, 'but you may name your price.'"

"Hooray!" shouted Amy, jumping up and down. She wrenched open the drawing-room door and called, "Champagne, Harris. At the double. Oh, Effy, we are in business again. Do not be so cross with me. If I had not pretended to be dying, then Delilah and Sir Charles might never have got together."

"We must go carefully," said Effy, "and not waste money on trifles."

"I agree," said Amy. "What a relief! We shall guard every penny from now on."

Harris brought in the champgane and the sisters toasted each other.

"Of course," said Effy, "they are prepared to pay a lot of money. It is mortifying not to have any decent jewellery and I did see such a pretty little sapphire necklace in Rundell and Bridges last month. A mere trifle."

"Buy it!" cried Amy, waving her hand and knocking over the champagne bottle.

"How clumsy you are," said Effy. "What will our new charge think of us? The daughter of dainty little Georgiana. She will be a delicate fairy-like creature and not a great hulking brute like you, Amy. I admit you did very well with Delilah. But you must allow me to take this delicate creature in hand.

"As you will," said Amy sourly. "As you will."